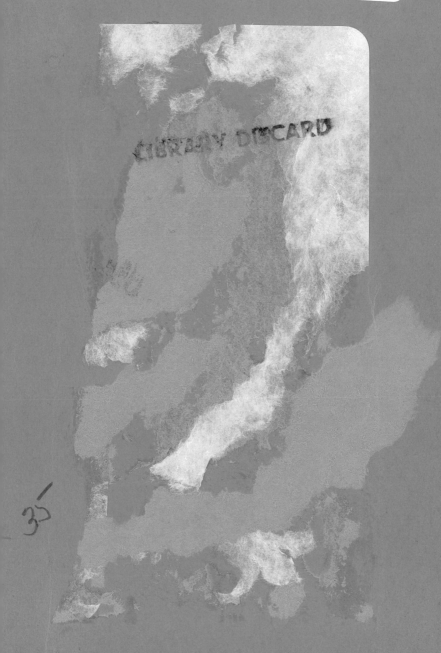

SECOND BREATH

Jan Beneš

second breath

Translated from the Czech by Michael Montgomery

The Orion Press, New York, 1969

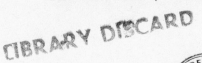

For J.M.

ET IN ARCADIA EGO

I do not deem it necessary to declare that the characters in this story have no counterparts in real life. The world is so small that —wrongly—it would prove me a liar. But the characters in this novel really are products of the author's imagination, set into an action that he does not consider improbable as a situation in life. The story also has no guilty parties—only people with whom one can agree or disagree. These views are, of course, a matter for each individual reader. The author, in his character of narrator, cannot urge the adoption of any particular point of view. He is therefore able to declare, too, that, insofar as anyone feels damaged by his story, he is affected merely by a subjective feeling, the roots of which mean nothing to the author. He does not intend to answer for it.

J. B.

Most, May 1960
Prague, September 1962—March 1963

CONTENTS

one the knight's domain 1

two colorless incident 25

three roll call 45

four happenings 81

five high noon 105

six final reckoning 149

Good and evil tongues assert
    that evil is perfect.
Thus falsehood and negation make life
    hate itself.

—*Paul Eluard*

the knight's domain

The barred turnstile welded out of profiled building steel slowly and clankily let them through into the camp. Only one man at a time entered the angle formed by its arms, and so it went on slowly, too slowly even, although it was a standing practice, something of a sport, too, to try and rush through the device so quickly that it spun at a mad rate, and the grating of the arms on the metal frame sounded like a machine gun. Only the escort guards did not like this. Slowness was what mattered to them. The prisoners had to march slowly enough for the guards to be able to count them. Like the camp guard shift, the escort were going off duty—and they were responsible for returning all prisoners to the camp. They showed a conscientious concern about it. This was their mission, and, apart from a few exceptions, none of the guards took it lightly. After all, they had live rounds in their guns, and every one of them had seen a dead prisoner before; cases of desperate and unsuccessful attempts to escape were documented by the photographs on the notice boards in their common room. There were orders, regulations, and instructions for carrying them out. Orders derived from orders.

On either side of the clanking entrance stood a man in uniform, the one inside unarmed, the one outside armed, and another sat behind the glass of the gatehouse. Inside the boundary strip were the escort commander and the brigade leader, the prisoner in charge. All with the same fixed gaze and the murmur of numbers on their lips. Their raised index fingers jerked as they counted the men. They were all counting. They were all responsible.

The prisoners came back from the mine dirty, still black from the coal, tired, hungry, and squinting half-blinded into the glow of the midday sun. The breakers and all the others who worked in the wind at the bottom of the shaft were dressed in winter-weight padded jackets with yellow warning stripes; this was acetone, which did not pick up coal dust, and it formed islands of brightness on their baggy clothes. Most of the shift, however, were wearing only linen mining clothes of an indeterminate green with blue bands stitched on along the seams. On the trousers like the stripes of a Salvation Army general, and on the jacket down the middle of the back. All still wearing their helmets, which they took off when they were about to enter the steel turnstile and pass before the eyes of the guards. It was their duty to take their hats off to a guard—and if anyone forgot, the sergeant in the gatehouse reminded him in no uncertain terms. He only needed to release the pedal with which he controlled the lock of the turnstile, and the rushing man would bang his head on the bars, which suddenly stopped turning. This meant, of course, that the prisoner behind him had to stop, too, then another and another, a whole long line right back to the trucks with the boxlike bodies and metal-covered windows, in which they were taken to and from work.

Whenever the regular clanking of the gate was disturbed, it also meant that the man in the gate at that moment attracted the attention of everyone; above all, of the guards, those in the escort and those on camp duty. This was not a thing that any of the men with the blue bands or the yellow stripes would have wanted. Being unforgettable causes difficulties, and only men who, as it were, are not there have any hope of sliding through life without blemish.

Small, gray, inconspicuous, insignificant, and forgettable little mice are destined to survive the cat.

But the gate banged almost every time, in every shift; newcomers would arrive by the regular weekly transport, with a shorter or longer stay in prison behind them before they were transported to the camp. But here there were different rules, a different regime, a different world, different people, different reasons for suicide or for living on, and you had to absorb everything new in such a way that you did what was required automatically and without thinking. For although it might appear that there was only one prison life, one state of being forced to live behind bars or wire, there in fact existed many differences, even though everywhere there were days when you had to eat beans or peas, everywhere there were tin plates to eat from, everywhere some kind of bars, and letters with the censor's stamp, and everywhere—like anywhere in the world—the truth belonged to those who possessed it. Those who had the power and the opportunity to declare that it was the truth.

That spring noon, the gate banged only once, and this was, of course, caused by a newcomer, a newt, a nestling, the greenhorn Vojda, 59 77, who had only arrived the day before in the latest transport and had also been immediately conspicuous because of his officer's uniform. Perhaps the whole camp pointed at him when the weekly delivery of fresh jailbirds, the wretched herd of dirt-stained civilians, was led in a straggling line of twos from the gate to sick bay and the store, where the barber and the storekeeper turned them into men worthy of re-education.

He banged his head against the bars so violently that he almost bounced off again. Then he stood for a long while (during which the man behind him ran into his back), not knowing what to do, as the band on the jacket of the man in front, which he had had constantly in reach, now suddenly disappeared somewhere into the distance. He was imprisoned between the arms of the turnstile, polished by the hands of prisoners, and he had made another *faux pas* in life that marked him out.

"*Cap!*" the brigade leader bawled at him, even though it was really a helmet.

"*Cap!*" shrieked an irritated chorus of many other voices in the crowd behind him. "*Cap off!*"

Vojda took it off as fast as the confined space of the gate permitted, the uniformed man in the gatehouse nodded his head and depressed the pedal, the prisoner behind Vojda grasped the free wing of the turnstile, and the ritual of coming in and counting was able to proceed.

"You idiot," said one of the men in the crowd behind to Vojda, one of those who had been shrieking a moment before. This was an excellent opportunity to say something like this—something that emphasized your own wisdom, experience, and knowledge of life. "You damned green mixed-up idiot of a newt!"

"He's a new one, sir," the brigade leader explained apologetically to the escort commander. But the latter only moved his head slightly as a sign that he had heard and understood, that he had reckoned on something of the sort. Vojda was the forty-sixth man to enter the camp, and the escort commander did not want to forget the number. There were 122 people in this shift today, and the escort commander, even though he was considered one of the most decent guards (at least from the prisoners' point of view), felt he was not living in vain only when the count came out right without having to be repeated.

Between the wire and the first huts of the camp was a small space, the "small parade ground," where the prisoners formed in ranks of five. One hundred and twenty men in ranks of five is not in fact all that much. An irregularly lined-up formation of curious volunteers straight out of some South American revolution. They looked at the sun, at the three lines of wire and the wooden fence daubed with tar paint that hid them from outside observation and at the same time hid the world from them. The country outside had disappeared. Only the sky remained and the administration hut behind their backs. The large plate-glass window of the nearest watchtower with its shooting slit above the floor. A large, backward-sloping display window, in fact, behind which they could imagine the leather straps of a belted jailer.

An older prisoner, tall and rather conspicuous in this dirty congregation, fell in behind Vojda. His hands and face were quite clean and unmarked and betrayed a more privileged position in the mine. A place where you did not get too dirty, where there were opportunities enough to wash and where you were also spared the battle for warm water that awaited all the others at the camp. When the space around him and Vojda had filled up, he took a small parcel tied up with wire from under his arm and showed it to Vojda: "If they pick me out, take this from me!"

There were no guards below ground. They only guarded the exits, and in the pits the prisoners worked side by side with civilian miners. Food, liquor, cigarettes, and also letters traveled via these civilian miners. Through them ran the supply route from the prisoners' families. Some of them wanted to help and took the risk. Some said they wanted to help and stole in the process. There had been more than one authenticated incident of a miner extorting things from a family left alone, old parents or a waiting fiancée. . . . But this was the supply route. A known possibility. The inspection after their return from work was designed to block it or at least to limit it.

The escort guards meanwhile left their weapons in the gatehouse and passed through the turnstile without taking their caps off. The inspection was their job, and, provided there had been no

denunciation, most of them only carried it out cursorily. It marked
the definite end of their duty. Soon they would be sitting down at
the table beside the wife to whom they gave their pay, and she
would scold the children who greeted them and climbed on to their
knees and played with the golden buttons on their uniforms:

*Now, children, leave Daddy alone. He's just finished work. And
he's tired!*

They took up position in front of the shift. One even walked
around the back of it (this, too, was part of the ritual). And each
one of them at random pointed at a rank of five. There had been no
denunciation today, which obliged them to carry out a full-scale
inspection. To act with too much certainty meant betraying the
informer. It was always someone who was able to give a parallel
report to the commandant. The escort knew on which side their
bread was buttered, whatever they may have thought in the
process. They had not the remotest desire to exchange their golden-
buttoned uniforms for suits with a blue band.

When one of the escort pointed to the rank of Vojda's neighbor
with the clean face, the first man marched forward without a word.
By chance, however, the prisoner in the second row had just fixed
his dreamy gaze somewhere in the sky and was staring in yearning
daydream and blinking at the sun, so that for concentration, for
sheer concentration, he failed to notice the gesture of command
from the escort, and the man with the clean face thus gained the
fraction of a second he needed to pass the parcel to Vojda. To a
Vojda, however, who had not yet had time to realize what the
man's words had meant, to a Vojda who had just completed his
first shift at the pit and his first day in the camp and who had also
just seen the camp for the first time in daylight . . . The parcel
fell to the ground and remained lying in the blank file left by the
departure of the five. Before one of the prisoners could pick it up or
at least kick it aside, the guard walking behind the parade leapt
for it.

"Whose is this?" He held his find by the end of the wire and rushed around to the front of the parade with it. *"Whose is this?"* His Adam's apple moved up and down. He stood in front of the file that had fallen out, and with the triumph of a little man who has shown that the world deserves him, he bawled: *"Whose is it? Come on! Quickly!"*

The escort guard turned around somewhat sourly. He was, after all, the one who had withdrawn this file for inspection. The prisoners looked indifferently into the distance, and the escort commander, up to now standing inactive beside the brigade leader, came up to the group that had formed and took the parcel into his hands.

"It was lying over there!" The guard pointed to the gap in the ranks. He was young and had somewhat long upper teeth. When his mouth was closed, they hung out between his lips and had given rise to the nickname Toothy, which was also used by his comrades-in-arms. He pointed to the spot at Vojda's feet: "There!"

The escort commander unwrapped the parcel slowly and without saying a word. Inside, wrapped in several layers of old newspaper, were a piece of reddish sausage and three tiny gherkins. He held it all on the flat of his hand amid the unwrapped paper. This looked ridiculous, and he was aware of it. A grown man searching for a few ounces of sausage and three little gherkins. He cast his eyes over the spot that Toothy pointed out and looked at the man with the washed face.

"Is this *yours?*"

"Yes."

"You *know* it is forbidden to bring anything into the camp?"

The man remained silent for a moment and looked at the meat and the little gherkins. There was no greater sin for a prisoner than to have even one finger in the world of freedom. To attempt to achieve the slightest independence. This tiny amount of food had been for his friend in sick bay.

The escort commander waved his outstretched hand that held
the paper. He was still clutching the untied piece of white wire in it,
too.

"Well, do you know or don't you?"

"Yes," said the man.

They looked at one another for a moment. The vague, tall man
with the clean face and the escort commander strapped up in his
leather harness, his pistol holster open and without its gun, which
he had left outside the wire in the gatehouse.

"Name?"

"Dobrovský," the prisoner said. "Number 77."

"Good Lord!" The escort commander straightened his shoulders. Number 77 meant the very beginning of the camp; it aroused
a feeling akin to respect. It was many, many years old, and came
from a time when this escort guard was still far away from being a
man in uniform and doubtless did not yet guess that places like this
camp existed anywhere on earth. He turned, marched slowly to the
gate, thrust his hand through somewhere outside, and said: "Take
this for the dogs!"

The sausage disappeared outside. He returned to Dobrovský
with the gherkins, the paper, and the wire. For perhaps a second,
he did not know what to do with it all. In the end, he leaned back
as though he were about to throw a grenade and hurled the gherkins one after another somewhere far beyond the death strip and
the fence painted with tar paint. Then he walked to the basket at
the door of the administration hut, crumpled up the paper and wire
and threw them inside. Finally, he came back and stood in front of
Dobrovský and looked up at him. The prisoner was taller than he
was.

"Who gave it to you?"

The man shrugged his shoulders and smiled faintly. To ask a
prisoner with the number 77 something like that! He opened his

mouth to reply, but the escort commander anticipated him:

"You found it! You came across it by chance, among the coal, eh?"

"Someone put it into my jacket, sir!"

That silence. What have we to say to one another, sir, the two of us, you and I? We both know it all. We both know our way about the camp. We know who we are and where we are, don't we? Sorry, sir, I think you're quite nice, we all do. . . . The escort commander could read all this out of the reply. He threw up his hands and took out a notebook and pencil. He took a few unnecessary steps.

"Why the hell didn't you eat it down below!"

But this was a rhetorical question, and Dobrovský did not attempt to reply to it. What could he explain to the escort commander about his friend in sick bay? . . . It is forbidden! Could the escort guard be interested in anything beyond this?

"Dobrovský, you will report to me!"

"Yes, sir!" replied the clean prisoner and again gave a barely perceptible smile.

The inspection was over. This time, none of the guards carried out a more thorough inspection, no surprise finds or any other success, apart from the piece of sausage and the three little gherkins. The discovery of the parcel had satisfied them, though it was regrettable that the finder had had to be Toothy, who did not belong to the escort, but was on camp duty. This did not give a good impression, and they liked Toothy all the less for it. The five returned to their places in the scattered formation of South American revolutionary volunteers, and the only incident was when one of the escort, Staff Sergeant Fousek, stopped the prisoner Günther and pointed to the toe of his boot, where his flapping sole formed a shark's jaw with rusty nails in place of teeth.

"Get that mended, man!" he said. "Or you'll find yourself paying for it!" Forfeiting the part of his earnings that were allowed to him could also be used as part of a prisoner's re-education. "Don't let me see you with that tomorrow!"

And Günther replied: "Yes, sir, but it only happened on the shift today."

Fousek accepted this answer. It was acceptable—and, anyway, the rest of the escort had already gone back out through the turnstile and had taken their pistols and automatic weapons from the gatehouse window and were walking in a group toward the common room and the bus stop. He had cautioned Günther out of sheer decency. The whole camp could confirm that Fousek was not a bastard. No one could say that Fousek had tried to catch him off guard or make life difficult for him.

There was a soft buzz of conversation among the shift. Dobrovský, who had dropped the parcel of sausage, did not speak. Vojda did not speak either. Several times, he took a breath and almost tried to say something, but the frosty, dead silence and the frosty, dead looks always robbed him of his courage. He had spent the three weeks before his arrival at the camp in prison awaiting trial. He tried to think of the sun, of his coal-stained hands. He did not succeed. He knew that the soft whisper was all about him. He heard a voice behind him hissing: "They'll give you the parcel now that you've been a good boy!"

Vojda turned to Dobrovský, although the hissing had not come from his lips.

"I didn't know. . . . I didn't do it on purpose!"

Dobrovský remained silent.

"Really! It's true!"

They were now waiting for the shift commander to arrive. The change-over took place between the guards somewhere inside the gatehouse, but they knew that the commander must come, recount the ranks of five, and order them to dismiss from the small parade ground to the camp. The brigade leader would give his report. But

they were in no hurry. Not only because the sun, which was precious to them, happened to be shining. They were patient. They
had learned to be patient. Impatience is the only cardinal human
sin. These men were patient. Therein lay their only strength, the
only morale that enabled them to face up to the malevolence of
fate.

At last, after a few minutes, the gate banged again, this time
briefly and once only, and the shift commander entered the camp.
They all let out a protracted sigh. The Rider, also known as the
Knight (the chess variety), was on duty. A fat, belted senior lieutenant with a bulging dropsical stomach, and the eyes, complexion,
and hair of an albino.

Of course, just like the prisoners, he, too, had a name and some
unrevealed fate. Years spent over a box of colored bricks and Dis-
neyesque pictures of Snow White in her glass coffin. A time when he
had existed only as an embryo and a hope without form. A time
when he had dreamed that he would get rid of his corpulence and
become an outstanding sportsman, a man whose name was in all
the newspapers, who was known from hundreds of photographs,
from radio and television. But by this time he had lost everything,
and he was left with only the nickname Rider or Knight, acquired
because he always wore high boots, and his short, thin, and slightly
bandy legs looked particularly grotesque in view of his bulging
stomach. His small, Prussian-cropped head (the smallest cap size
in camp) commanded a body that weighed more than 250 pounds.
He was known to have difficulties with mathematics (those eternal
discrepancies in the counting) and to have come to this camp
as a punishment, because, at some other camp, he had had two
prisoners tied up by the wrists—this had been done publicly, so
there was proof of his action. He knew that everyone knew; his
reputation had preceded him long ago, in that mysterious way that
the guards were always seeking to uncover, but which would never
be revealed in concrete terms because it rested on the principle of

chance and operated through common bonds that were beyond the
bounds of logic. Friendship, curiosity, visitors to prisoners who
knew relatives of other prisoners, prisoners migrating from camp to
camp. The fortuitously uttered word of an investigator trying to
demonstrate that he had moral and human interests at heart. Immediately, from the very first day the Knight had appeared here,
everyone had known it was him. *Him*, the Knight, the lieutenant
who, according to the rumor from the camp where he had had the
two prisoners hung up by the wrists and dislocated their shoulders
in the process, suffered from literal-mindedness. Everyone knew
which camp it had been, and everyone also knew the lieutenant's
real name. It was Černý, but the nickname described him more
perfectly than any real name, better than the most perfectly filed
cadre material or sociopsychological report. The worst of it was
that he realized this. He was the Knight, and all his running about
the camp was just a game that he was not intended to understand.
The Knight.

The very first day after he arrived, he had furthermore given
the whole camp a demonstration of the things he was reputed to be
capable of. After the afternoon count, he had made all the shifts
march on the concrete area that still remained from the times when
the Germans had kept Russian prisoners here during the war. True,
marching in itself was nothing out of the ordinary. But he had also
ordered them to sing. The camp had never known anything like
it—and old inmates reminiscing were able to say pensively: "You
see! Just you wait, *this one* will end up by turning the whole camp
sour. *Then* you'll see something!"

The Knight had arrived some time at the beginning of autumn,
and today—the day he made them stand on the small parade
ground in order to test their patience and strengthen what was
none too accurately called discipline—it was already the beginning
of April. One of the first sunny days, especially precious in this
region. A newcomer, the former air-force lieutenant Vojda, had for-

gotten to remove his helmet in the gateway. Günther, the German who did not speak a word of German, had a torn sole on his boot. And the tough old jailbird Dobrovský was to report to the commander, because he had been caught with a piece of sausage and three little green gherkins. It was the beginning of April. The nights were still cold, but it was warm in the daytime, and if the sun happened to be shining, as it was now, the world looked quite pleasant. With waiting came sleepiness and thoughts of the girls with whom they had lain in the sun, long ago, when they were still free men.

As the Knight came in, the prisoners' sigh did not escape him. It did not signify relief, but distress and disappointment. The realization that they all had to be on their guard until lights-out and keep out of the way. The Knight heard the sigh and was satisfied. This was the last, or nearly the last, of the feelings he still had left in life, and he thought he was entitled to it at the expense of people who had trousers with Vatican stripes and blue bands down the middle of their backs. He was even proud of it. He had the peak of his cap well forward and bore his birdlike head, with the pale eyes and the sparse white hair, painfully straight.

Helmet in hand, the brigade leader made his report on the strength of the shift and any exceptional occurrences—one broken hand, otherwise everything in perfect order.

The lieutenant listened to the report, standing almost at attention, though, of course, without removing his cap or saluting. He stepped nearer and gave the brigade leader some instructions in a whisper. Then, suddenly, he noticed some movement among the prisoners; someone had scraped his foot or coughed. He interrupted himself nervously, rushed several steps toward the spot where he had noticed the disturbance, and shouted: *"What's going on here?"*

Immediately, everything stood still. Silence fell—a dead calm that satisfied the Knight. He returned to the brigade leader, who was waiting for him, helmet in hand, and repeated his orders of the day in a whisper. In a whisper, because everything the Knight did had to have an aura of secrecy about it.

"March off to the huts, no one to run on ahead, parade for lunch immediately. If there's any disorder, the whole shift will march for one hour!"

The brigade leader put his helmet on and gave the order to march. The shift turned right and marched around the corner of the administration hut onto the large parade ground and across the concrete strip to their own hut, number six. The Knight looked after them until the moment the brigade leader gave the order to dismiss in front of the hut. Then he went back out through the turnstile and disappeared into the gatehouse. A moment later, the camp public-address system rang with his muffled voice: "I order the cooks to serve lunch to the early shift Koh-i-noor! *I repeat!* lunch for the early shift Koh-i-noor!"

The guard on cookhouse duty was Bobo. A man who called himself a jailer. Just as it was necessary to keep out of the Knight's way, so it was possible to have a decent conversation with Bobo. Bobo was in a state of deep melancholy. He had originally wanted to be a military messenger. A kamikaze fastened into a leather suit and only starting to live at sixty miles an hour, but, by some chance, this had not happened. Bobo's dream of a roaring engine had not come true, and instead of the leather kamikaze suit, he had put on the green uniform of a jailer—which is not a pejorative term, but just a simple definition of a man's job, stating succinctly that he guards a jail, just as a teacher teaches, a worker works, and a smith runs his smithy.

Apart from a few packets of coffee and cans of food, a guitar and an English textbook had also been brought into the camp by the prisoners that day. The textbook by Havránek, a former pilot, who, because of his job, was still called Pilot, and the guitar by

Daniel, a small-town playboy. He brought it in tied to his back under his tunic, despite the considerable risk involved. A guitar is not some small trifle that you can pass to your neighbor behind your back, especially when it is tied on. There had also been the problem of wriggling through the gate with it. But he had managed.

Bobo stood in front of the cookhouse, the cooks leaned out of the open serving hatches, waiting, and the shift rushed along the corridors of the hut to get their tin plates from their rooms. Havránek was able to deposit the English textbook in his locker. Daniel was able to push his guitar out of sight under the bed. Both of them still had to falsify their permits, but that was a small matter, once the things were there. The guitar could be explained as being needed for the music circle. The textbook was quite small. A guitar, a textbook, coffee, tobacco, a bottle of beer, a couple of packs of cigarettes . . . all this, of course, had no value, and it was possible to get by without it, and all those who took the risk were, of course, more like desperadoes than good citizens, even though *here,* and this word was pronounced with special emphasis, *here* was the place where you were supposed to calm down. But *here* was also the place where a long line of people who had always been nothing less than good citizens revealed that they were in fact more like desperadoes than anything else, and that they wanted to be and had to be.

Because they were, of course, rogues and scoundrels who lived from their roguery just as others take their fill of bread or love or a combination of the two. But the great majority of people do not want to be rogues; they do not want to be anything but normal, simple people, until suddenly they find themselves in a situation that forces them to behave out of character despite their desires for simplicity and normality. Hope beckons them, and they succumb and turn into different people, just as a girl who has slept with a man can no longer be a girl who has not yet slept with a man, just as a man who has had his foot torn off by a train can no longer be the man he was before, just as a writer who lies for some reason can never again be a man who knows he has never lied, just as someone who has been beaten up keeps traces of the beating within himself long after the last bruise has faded from his body. Someone who has once somehow got himself on the other side of normality, whether by becoming a brilliant sculptor or a brilliant swindler, smuggler, or deadbeat; individual consciousness of having passed beyond a known boundary remains in him as long as he is still conscious that he exists, that somewhere some other life also exists. A farther shore, a place the boats sail to.

Soon there would no longer be a man nicknamed Pilot, but only an anonymous citizen (who, of course, would never again be trusted with an aircraft). Long after the bed he now slept on had had many other owners, while he himself lay over the splayed thighs of a woman, naturally a pretty one (he was the sort of man that women like), long after this, even though it would then be necessary to change the mattresses, and they would be changed and again destroyed by incessant use, dust, and fumigation against vermin, long after no one was left in the whole dormitory who knew his face and remembered that his real name was Havránek, his nickname would still live on here as well as the reminiscence: "Pilot used to sleep here, a man who once lived by flying a plane, and who used to say, when the camp boundary strip lit up in the evening:

'Whenever we were flying over here at night, I used to wonder what these strange squares of light were—well, now I know!' "

Apart from this, Pilot was also the constructor of a water heater for making tea or coffee, a secret heater, of course, which had been used in the days when it was forbidden to make hot drinks in the huts. Two forged plate-layer's bolts were pierced with a piece of rubber belting and connected to an electric wire. The bolts, the rubber, and the wire could be procured in the pit. Up by the lamp under the ceiling, a stretch of the electric conduit was stripped of its insulation, and the wire was hung up on it by its bent ends. When the bolts were immersed in a glass boiler full of water, this was enough to bring it to a boil in a few minutes. Only, all this was nothing but a fraction of the complex of things that would cause the concept of the man to be preserved in the name Pilot. The true reason lay in the fact that always, *always*, he had stood beyond the bounds of normality, even the unusual normality of prison conditions, that he was a man who did not waste words and who was in possession of himself, who did not wallow in ill-placed sentiment and reflection on future roguery that would astonish the world.

They ate lunch, still dirty and swathed in coal dust (except for Dobrovský and one or two other lucky ones), and only then did they hang their helmets and the indeterminate green mining clothes with blue bands at the heads of their bunks and go off to the showers (five bent pipes with a garden sieve at the end for 120 miners). They washed the sweat and weariness off themselves, and they swilled the remains of the lunch from their tin plates. They were able to feel that they now had the worst part of the day behind them. The satisfied, clean feeling of a man who has been washed. The violent murderer just as much as the swindler. Havránek, closed up and taciturn as Mephistopheles, just as much as the town playboy Daniel, who had been locked up because the girl he made love to had not been old enough for the law to be able to ignore their love-making. It all came out when the girl got pregnant, and Daniel, who was then eighteen, did not want to marry her. It all came out—a girl of tender years wanted to get married because she was pregnant. It all came out—the authorities had already arranged everything else, and the wedding was canceled. Daniel went to prison rather than go to the town hall. The law was the law, and now he was suffering the consequences of his transgression. The girl had meantime born him a son, and it was now up to Daniel to show, by good behavior and hard work, that he was sufficiently re-educated, that he would never again be a menace to society, and that he could be released after serving half the sentence in an obedient and disciplined manner; released on parole, of course, so that society could have some security. Trust and prove! For the law is the law, and the law is the expression of the common will, which, allegedly, does not want to have fifteen-year-old mothers. Perhaps because of this, Daniel had been able to bring a guitar into the camp tied to his back. Perhaps because of this—smuggling in a guitar was not, of course, disciplined behavior. Perhaps because of this.

It had been Vojda's first shift. He had mined for the first time, and for the first time, too, he had had to wash coal off himself. He did it badly—he lacked the routine. Flecks of black remained around his eyes, in the folds and lines on his face, in his ears and nostrils. He looked like a strange, half-made-up clown, surprised with part of his everyday face somewhere behind the scenes, or like the *maîtresse* of some brothel after an orgy lasting a week. Like every newcomer, he was, of course, dependent on someone lending him soap and voluntarily taking care of him and advising him, just as they had shouted *cap* at him when he forgot to take his helmet off to the guard at the turnstile. But the Dobrovský incident had placed him behind a wall of suspicion, and he was aware of it and felt all the more lonely and ignored.

Vojda, too, had been a pilot, until quite recently—a pilot first-class and a man highly placed in the hierarchy of constructed revolution that had put Havránek into jail when Vojda was still a boy. He, of course, had never been surprised about the illuminated squares down below. For him, they were part of reality. He had been withdrawn from the mainstream of life because of a man he had run over in his car a few days after the New Year. In his car

and with a by-no-means-small drop of alcohol in his blood. The
man had died, and Vojda had stopped flying. Today, he had mined
for the first time, he was washing off the grime of the pit for the first
time, and he was spitting out black phlegm for the first time. He
had three weeks behind him and another seventy-eight in front of
him. Altogether, nearly a year and a half, which was certainly time
enough to make sure he never again sat behind the wheel of a car
with alcohol inside him and knocked a man down and killed him.

He was not accustomed to being alone. At first, he had dreaded
this terrible blunder in his planned career. He had not been accustomed to being alone—not since he was fifteen and accepted for the
military academy, because of his spotless cadre origin, right up to
the last after-duty party that had ended with the crash. He knew
all about those squares down below—they were landmarks for nav-
igation—but he thought no more of it. He was only twenty-two, he
was a pilot first-class—and then along came this car accident. He
had dreaded the thought of living side by side with criminals who
had committed their crimes just as responsibly as he had flown.
Great hopes had been set on him, too, when he was still an embryo.
He, too, had the feeling of a man who was *different*—for he flew
airplanes and was used to living as part of a group at an air base.
He was not married, nor did he know any reason why he should
be—it clearly would not have helped him to achieve any of the
things he longed for. What is marriage? The great happiness of
solidarity, of a firm base from which we force our way through the
world, the immensity of abandoned egoism, the beautiful accident
of a love capable of bringing even stones to life—or a couple of
merry games for which we sell our freedom, a staff to support a
man unable and unwilling to admit his weakness and his fear, his
reluctance to go away without witnesses, memories, and relics, to
take away with him only his knowledge of the senselessness of it
all? Vojda was no blockhead, though they had been trying to make
him into one since he was fifteen. He was not a blockhead as far as

women were concerned. He had money, a car, a comfortable room
with a bath, and he was bathed in romanticism. But he was not
convinced that love was necessary. In his head, stored memories of
twelve-year-old fellow pupils and games of doctor mingled with his
experience with the forty-year-old wife of the airfield commandant.
The women warrant officers from the air-traffic control and other
ancillary services at the base used to say that he had lovely hair.
He felt satisfied by this. He looked after his hair.

After the first shock of prison, the filth, the nastiness, the despair, and the fear of the unknown, he was seized by the curiosity
of a child who goes camping for the first time in his life and looks
forward to telling his friends, who have not yet experienced anything like it, all about it when he gets back.

He was thus doubly regretful and afraid of the silence that
surrounded him after the incident of the parcel. Everything had
changed *again*. He came up against closed lips and ruthless hostile
faces. He was not accustomed to being alone, and would have simply exchanged the officers at the airfield for the people in the camp.
As far back as his twenty-two-year-old memory reached, he had
only listened to empty speeches about the collective and the joyous
present, about a more and more joyous present, and he had got
used to them. Now, recently, of course, he had also heard talk
about the chances of parole if there were no obstacles. . . . The
parcel was certainly an obstacle. An obstacle outside the bounds of
the Discipline-Work-Conduct triumvirate, which alone could guarantee that he would never again get drunk and sit behind the wheel
of a car with alcohol inside him. The parcel could mean nine
months of freedom or nine months in prison. And here, *here,* was
the place where you were supposed to work and calm down. Nine
months here or nine months outside the wire where Dobrovský's
gherkins had fallen. But Vojda had not forgotten to take the parcel
because he wanted to dissociate himself. He was awkward and for-
getful. He had always been a friendly sort, and he saw no reason

why he should not be now. Despite all the speeches about the present, and despite everything that was not talked about—indeed, just because it was not talked about—he sensed rather than knew that reality was something different from the more and more joyous present. His defense mechanism was to be a friendly sort. This was better than all the speeches he had ever heard. It was better than all the discipline and order in the world, even of a world that had raised him to the position of pilot first-class.

TWO

colorless incident

All men are born equal,
and that is the only honor
for all of us!

—Maxim Gorky, *Confessions*

by the time of the greatest scramble for water, Havránek was already long washed and ensconced in the atelier, a strange long room with one window, which, as necessary, was also occasionally called the self-improvement circle or the art center, depending on which of the guards was on duty at the time. It was in fact a dead end in the corridor, where, in the designer's original conception, the prisoners were supposed to clean their boots. In the designer's original conception, of course, each man in the hut was also supposed to have twelve cubic yards of space. At one time in the past, before some state occasion, when there had been a need for posters and placards, doors had been fitted across the corridor. Later a hole had been knocked through the wall to the chimney of the neighboring dormitory and the stones placed in the corner by the door. A long noodle with a mosaic floor, a couple of chairs, and two tables. It was no more pleasant here than in a suburban public lavatory. But it was possible to lock up this noodle of a room, to separate it from the camp around it. It locked, and the key to the door was held by the self-improvement man or by the art man, but Havránek's chum, his friend Jarda, always had a key. Jarda had once been an organizer, and several other things, too. Now, he was a prisoner and acted as something approaching Pilot's personal assistant. The atelier was their private life. Jarda had had to fight hard for the key and the rights that it automatically and inconspicuously conferred. He had managed it because he grasped that the task of the day was to *fool*, that this was, in general, the slogan of the age, and because he was backed by Pilot's experience. To *fool*, a word frequently used in jail, was and is in place here, *here*, and *here* also has a very precise meaning of its own. To *fool* means to get permission for a parcel. To *fool* means to achieve visits outside the normal times. To *fool* means the small victories in the fight against humiliation.

In Jarda's case, it had meant the letters of the slogans painted on brown paper. They had been devised by the guard in charge of education or by Jarda himself. The letters were always blue or red, and the background yellow, cadmium emulsion spread thickly with a mason's brush. The *fooling* also meant lunch or dinner without lining up and without the parade at the cookhouse (the excuse being the importance of painting the letters), but, above all, it meant the atelier, built by the fitting of old doors across the dead end in the corridor. Many, many such persuasive slogans had had to be painted on their knees before the commandant was convinced that such a room was really necessary, for all this was obviously necessary if the guards wanted to have their posters with red and blue letters on a yellow background. And, finally, the *fooling* also meant getting four buckets of coal a day for these few feet of corridor, for the atelier did not have, and did not need, a coal permit—it worked so closely with the guards in preparing their posters—while the ration for the dormitories was never more than a bucket a day, however many miners lived there and however severe the frosts.

Jarda, of course, did not use the atelier just for painting letters and obtaining coal, which was then transferred to the dormitories. It was, above all, an asylum of solitude and privacy, a place where forbidden things could be done with much less chance of disturbance, a place where he and Pilot locked themselves up to study, to make coffee, to live. In the dormitory, they both slept in the same row, and in the atelier, Pilot was teaching Jarda English. He was teaching him the English he had picked up in the RAF during the war, until one day he had realized that he had nothing more to teach him, that time had performed its work of destruction with him, too, and so he had got hold of the textbook through a civilian miner friend. On the quiet, of course. Anyone found with English word lists exposed himself to serious suspicion of sympathy toward England, which was after all a member of NATO, and such sympathies were not a sign of re-education. Discipline-Work-Conduct. Fortunately, neither Pilot nor Jarda wanted to convince anyone that they had been re-educated. They knew their own minds, and they wanted to have peace and quiet, a standard of their own as people expert in fooling, navigating this overcomplicated and none-too-normal world and triumphing over the unkindness of fate, even if only in a small way.

Pilot was just faking the censorship stamp on the title page of the smuggled textbook, and Jarda was painting under a blue INCREASE YOUR WORKING EFFORT the red letters YOU WILL SHOW BY YOUR WORK THAT YOU ARE . . . , and meanwhile he was going over the English words from a piece of paper pinned to the wood that served him as a drawing board.

cuff—*manžeta*

wife—*manželka*

ox—*vůl*

YOU WILL SHOW BY YOUR WORK THAT YOU ARE . . . He rested his template on the paper and carefully drew the brush along it. Tiny, running, angular drops formed on the back feet of the letters.

"English is the mother tongue of the English!" Then the brush stopped after the last word, THAT YOU ARE . . . He did not have the rest of the slogan penciled in in rough. He turned to Havránek: "Hey, what do you show by your work?"

Pilot shrugged his shoulders; he was completely engrossed in his counterfeiting. He was working hard and with great concentration, using a sharpened matchstick and paint made from powdered brick. It was better than real paint for faking stamps—it did not smudge.

Jarda put his brush down and began to rummage about in the mess on the table. He stopped repeating the words and began to curse softly. In his rage, he scattered a pile of rolled-up brown paper and odd pieces smeared with test strokes of his brush, boxes of pins and old newspapers.

"I had it written down here somewhere, straight from the education man. It was something about society."

It is said that there are good and bad people, just as there are good and bad jobs, and that the bad jobs are all those that are done without pleasure or even under duress out of the sheer necessity to work and earn a living. Work is supposed to be man's mission on earth.

But Jarda was not averse to painting the slogans, any more than Pilot was averse to faking the censorship stamp, even though for them both were sheer necessity here if they wanted a way of life that was at least a little tolerable and congenial. The painting of the slogans and the false stamp were ways of coming to terms with power without subjecting oneself to it. And it was a question, it is a question, of being in control of your own life, even though you know you cannot prevent your body from feeling hunger or longing for sleep. But this was just the way to satisfy yourself independently of everything in the camp that determined whether you ate enough or slept enough. A necessity limited only to the very bounds of necessity. A form of freedom. To remain independent and not to be afraid, even when it seemed there was nothing else you could do. With a measure of absolute indifference to whether the guards represented society, as they liked to say, or whether they only represented themselves. Indifference to whether they really happened to represent society. The Knight was not Bobo, and thus there could not be any *one* society when it was represented by two so different people. The censorship stamp could protect the English lessons from Bobo or one of the other decent guards. From the Knight or the education officer, nothing would have protected it. But the Knight and the education officer rarely carried out inspections personally. Freedom meant knowing what was needed. Pilot knew what was needed.

"Oh, you mustn't take it all so personally," he would say to Jarda in the days when they still needed to cheer one another up about such things. "You mustn't take it so personally, or you won't get away from it. Look at the Knight and all the others just as you look at the wire, the bars, and the locks. They are nothing more, and you can come to terms with them that way."

That was Pilot. Everything that made him the man he was. Letters from a beautiful woman, which he received and then burned, words he heard and yet did not obey.

It seemed that he never fought for anything and never demanded anything, nor did he in fact write pleading petitions with requests for one thing or another—he did not care about anything enough to humiliate himself for it. And yet, by some mysterious and imperceptible route, he had everything a man in a camp could want from life. No one knew why he had spent five or perhaps seven years here, although it was known that he only had a few months left to go. He was a taciturn and serious man, this Havránek, a bit of an eccentric, rather in the manner of the Jehovah's Witnesses, of the same make-up as they displayed when they held out obstinately over the long years in the camp—all because of a mere two years' military service, which they refused to do.

He had once been summoned before a board that decided whether a prisoner was sufficiently corrected—re-educated. The camp commandant himself had put Havránek's name forward. By this time, Pilot had been inside for many years, for more than half his sentence, a veteran of the camp from its first days, a man everyone knew.

Everyone summoned to appear was understandably nervous and keyed up, and the five prisoners who were taken there together with Pilot (the parole board held mass hearings. Why waste time on it, comrades?) were, in addition, filled with curiosity in case, when the evidence was read out, they might discover something about who this man Havránek really was, and what he had been sent here for. (I always wondered what those strange squares of light were.) Havránek, too, was a little curious. He had once admittedly had a trial of sorts, but he had never had the indictment in his hands and had never received the verdict in writing.

Only before the actual proceedings started, the chairman of the parole board had asked everyone brought before it whether they had anything to say, any point they wished to stress. They asked Havránek, too, and told him again that it had been the commandant himself, *the commandant himself,* who had put his name forward for parole—on the grounds of good work and exemplary conduct.

Havránek nodded that he would like to say something, that he had something on his mind, and the chairman, a tractor driver who had done a one-year law course, and a barber by trade before he had become a tractor driver, had motioned him to say what he had to say now. Prisoners who enjoyed the commandant's favor were treated with mercy, and the chairman, just like Havránek, knew that the commandant did not hand out his favor just like that, that it was an instruction from somewhere *above,* from the same place and perhaps even from the same man who had once decided on Havránek's submersion in the camp. They expected the usual words for this place and time. Expressions of patriotism, of loyalty to the system, and of good intentions for the future.

But Pilot had cleared his throat and said he would like the

woman stenographer to plug her ears, because what he was going to
say was not intended for her or for any woman at all, but those
gentlemen there . . . and he pointed his finger along the line, *that
one* (the first judge from the people, the assessor concealing under
his robes a leather jerkin whose cuffs could be seen, a bus driver by
profession), *that one* (the chairman of the board, the barber, tractor driver, and lawyer with a year's postal training behind him,
asserting himself as the transmission belt of Party policy in the
legal system), and *that one* (a cow-tender from a state farm a few
miles away)—these gentlemen could kindly kiss his ass, because he
had never known and still did not know what good parole would be
to him when he had never known and still did not know the reason
he had been in the camp for all these years.

This was, of course, contempt of court, but it was no longer the
year in which Pilot had been sentenced; Stalin had died long ago,
and all values were shifting. He got thirty days in solitary confinement.

He came back a month later, thinner for the experience—food
had been served only every third day—and somewhat more talka-
tive after a month of solitary confinement, and with his hair longer
than usual. He paraded for work again the next day, and, surpris-
ingly, by a mysterious stroke of fate, his "niche" had been kept
open for him, his plum job, his relatively comfortable position as
driver of the mine engine. Whenever anyone asked him why on
earth he had insulted the court when it was in the cards that he
would be going home, he replied lazily that he had not had any
reason for not insulting the court.

Every day after the shift, or before if it was an afternoon shift,
he and Jarda would lock themselves in the atelier. Jarda studied
and Pilot went over their English lessons, and sometimes he would
throw in a story from the war years. They brewed the forbidden
coffee and watched the bread liquor fermenting in the gherkin bottle. One day, Pilot had decided that he did not know as much Eng-

lish as he should, and he had written a letter, perhaps to the beautiful woman who corresponded with him and also occasionally came to visit him. He had written the letter and smuggled it from the camp to the mine inside his leggings. A week later, he had brought the textbook back from the mine, strapped behind his belt and covered by his loose tunic with its blue band, and he was now forging the censorship stamp with a sharpened match and paint made from crushed brick. Real paint could be smudged. Once the little pieces of brick dust had been blown off the paper, a permanent impression would remain, just like the real stamp.

Jarda eventually found the text of the slogan in the jumble on the table and pinned it beside the English word list; he took the template and brush into his right hand and carefully shook the paint can several times with his left. Then he put it down, stirred it experimentally a few more times with the brush, passed the template into his free hand, put it to the paper, and, deftly and rapidly, without any rough outline in pencil, he added the end of the slogan on the yellow background:

. . . THAT YOU ARE WORTHY TO BECOME A FULLY FLEDGED MEMBER OF HUMAN SOCIETY. "Fully fledged" was Jarda's own addition; the education officer's slogan had not contained these words. He shook the brush out onto a rag and, for safety's sake, used it to soak up two or three angular drips that were gathering at the ends of letters. Then, with satisfaction, he threw the implements down into the mess of paper and said: "English is the mother tongue of the English."

Havránek was still fussing over his false stamp and was about to point out his not-quite-correct pronunciation when there was a knock at the door.

For a moment, they merely straightened up and remained motionless. But in the pause between the first and the second knock (there were three altogether), Pilot managed to place a piece of blotting paper between the pages over the wet stamp and to thrust the textbook behind the window ledge. In a flash, Jarda had torn the word list from the board. Only then did they both look at the door. They did all this quite automatically, rather as other people brush fluff from their sleeve or blow their noses, even though they had only met in the camp and had previously lived in completely different places and in completely different ways. Pilot with a woman who was pretty (lips, breasts, thighs, and legs); Jarda with a father and mother who had not yet realized that their son was grown up.

Pilot took a broken pencil and began to stir the can of paint. Stirring paint was a reason that justified the presence in the atelier even of people who could not paint red and blue letters.

"Who is it?" asked Jarda. He had to. He had left the key blocking the lock, and it could be seen plainly from the outside.

"WHO IS IT?" he asked again when there was no reply to his first challenge, and his voice was less mild and patient.

The man at the other side of the door turned the handle and tried to open it. It was only when he saw that the door would not give that he said: "Excuse me, is Comrade Havránek there?"

Comrade?

Jarda glanced at Pilot, and Pilot shrugged his shoulders. They had both known since the second knock that there was no one outside from whom they needed to hide the book and the word list.

"He's here. What do you want?" By now, Jarda was speaking with a little more coarseness in his voice. He walked over to the door, and because they had both been annoyed by the word "Comrade" (Jarda, of course, a little more than Pilot), he turned the key and wrenched the door open violently, like a film detective opening the door of a hide-out where he is going to arrest a dangerous murderer, like a man on the verge of anger which is going to burst out in full force in a moment. Perhaps he really was angry. About the disturbance, the moment of uncertainty, the unnecessary work they had had in clearing away the traces of the English lesson. Jarda did occasionally get angry. This was one of the ways in which he differed from Havránek. Pilot never lost his temper. And he did not share Jarda's mood at this moment either. He stood by the window, resting his back against the wall, one leg crossed over the other; he held the broken pencil in his hand and dabbled with it in the can of blue paint.

At the door stood Vojda, a little breathless and clearly prepared for a "What the hell" or "Damn." Vojda, whom they remembered from the previous day when the transport of newcomers marched from the gate to sick bay as the man in air-force uniform. . . . Now he stood before them in a two-piece suit of refined hemp with tin buttons inherited from the Wehrmacht, and in a cap that was too big for him, like most of the caps issued in this little world; he had had to draw it together over his brow with a piece of binding wire. It now resembled an Aztec headband. When he had marched through the camp in his officer's uniform, he had aroused a little *Schadenfreude*. There was a fair number of former soldiers in the camp, and an officer's uniform evoked pleasant associations. So you've got it, too, my lad. They did not understand it as a disaster, but as their edification. He had once been set above them, and now suddenly they were at the same level and had the same superiors.

Jarda and, of course, Pilot, too, remembered Vojda from the incident at the turnstile. Although Jarda had no reason for it, he took a step back and let Vojda in without a word. Pilot was still standing at his place by the window, looking like a figure in some tableau—unmoved and immovable as an American film cowboy. He was still holding the paint can in his hand and the piece of broken pencil with which he was stirring. Vojda came in and remained standing half a step over the threshold of the opened door. They were all waiting for some open-sesame which would get them out of this situation. Vojda full of shame, and Pilot and Jarda full of the suspicion of a child who has already experienced what it is to touch a hot stove. Then the curiosity in them—if such a term can be applied to what interested them about Vojda—triumphed. The knowledge that he was the nearest of them in time to some sort of life, the life that they had known and perhaps even not prized too highly, because it struck them as everyday and normal. He was near, the nearest of them to a woman's breasts which he could touch and kiss, which he had certainly kissed. That was freedom, love, perhaps, everything they knew, everything they knew existed, but they still wanted to hear it all again and again. Camp life was so unchanging; there was rarely anything new. They wanted—Jarda more than Pilot—to hear it, eagerly even, despite the fact that it was all the same and that these were all other men's adventures that meant nothing at all. The only thing that really matters is to find a pathway between power and the obligations it imposes on us, and the measure of freedom that we consider indispensable in order to live.

"Come on in!" said Jarda.

Vojda advanced another half step, but again not far enough to enable the door to be closed.

"I heard"—he ran his hand uncertainly over his face, a movement that had accompanied him since childhood—"that one of you is a pilot." He coughed. "Havránek?" Not knowing which of the two men in the room was Havránek, he looked hesitantly first at Jarda, who was standing with his hand on the door handle, and then at Pilot, who was leaning his back on the window ledge, still holding the paint can and the pencil stump. They looked at one another.

"I'm Havránek."

If up to now Jarda had been unable to understand why he had let Vojda in and had not thrown him out, he now yielded to Pilot's authority and said in a quite friendly tone:

"Come in, so I can lock up again!"

Vojda advanced another half step and addressed Havránek again: "They told me you were a pilot, too."

Pilot, too, remembered Vojda's air-force uniform. But he had an even lower number than Dobrovský. A number from the first transport of that year long ago when the first prisoners appeared in the camp after the Russian prisoners of war. He dabbled indifferently in the paint with the pencil.

"I used to fly with Czechoslovak Airlines. It's a terribly long time ago now. It's stopped being true any more."

Vojda raised his hands to his chest.

"I thought, I had an idea—perhaps we have some friends in common." He sensed how wretched and unconvincing his reason was. It was a bad sentence, and he was ashamed of it. It was not convincing. It did not attract friends.

It was quiet again. Vojda began to look uncertainly at the poster with the letters. Havránek tightened one corner of his mouth and mixed the paint thoroughly.

"It's difficult," he said after a while. "It's all so terribly long ago now." He again surveyed Vojda in his wretched prison uniform, the kind that only a newcomer without connections and experience can draw from the stores; he felt something akin to pity, and perhaps also a gust of professional solidarity. He smiled.

"We're colleagues—but for God's sake don't call me Comrade again. It's not used here. If you get mixed up in front of a guard, he'll punish you."

Vojda again steadied himself with a movement of his hand across his face.

"It's just habit, I do it out of habit. Don't be angry!" He was glad there was no longer silence around him. Before him stood a pilot, and they were linked by the brotherhood of the joy-stick, the control column. Both of them had held it; both had looked at the world from above. Both had experienced their moments of nervousness in the pit of the stomach.

"I'm not angry," Pilot replied. He felt no need to fraternize. That incident with the parcel of sausage. "I'm not telling you this because I'm angry, but you seem to be having bad luck right from the start. I know what it's like." He stabbed the pencil into the paint with an air of finality and set the can down on the edge of the table. He took a tobacco tin and a roll of papers from his pocket. Slowly, he began to roll himself a cigarette. He noticed Vojda's look. Newcomers in the camp were always like nonswimmers thrown into a river, and always lacked the smoking habit. He held out his hand to him with the tobacco tin.

"Want one?"

Vojda shook his head.

"I don't smoke. It's just that I've never seen anyone rolling cigarettes before."

"You'll save money if you don't have to smoke," said Jarda. This was a universal truth on which they could agree. But the incident of Dobrovský's parcel stuck in Jarda, too, like a knife. He spoke in the tones of a slightly worried man.

Pilot at last finished rolling his cigarette, handed the tobacco tin to Jarda, and lit up.

"Once people form an opinion of you, you'll find it difficult to get rid of it, you know."

Vojda felt the narrow and longed-for link of the control column fading away beyond his grasp. From lunchtime up to the moment he set out to find Pilot in the atelier, he had sat in the dormitory and had to listen to remarks about informants, *provocateurs*, and spies who came to a bad end. Stories of the evil fates that overtook them in the dark passages of the mine. Everyone around needed, often for years on end, someone to vent his hate on. And now they could hate him with some reason. They had to. Some of them harshly and in public. Others sarcastically: *Just you be nice and good, and sir will let you go home.* Dobrovský had listened to his apology, said yes, and turned his back on him.

"That matter of the parcel," Vojda croaked in an undertone. "I'm terribly sorry about it, but I didn't do it deliberately. Really!"

Havránek and Jarda exchanged a glance. Jarda's cigarette was now made, too, and he lit it. The tobacco tin and papers went back into Pilot's pocket.

"What's new outside?" asked Jarda.

Vojda shrugged his shoulders, not knowing what to say.

"Outside? Nothing. I don't know."

Havránek turned the tobacco tin over in his pocket. He held it by the edge, rested it against his body, and ran his fingers along it right to the other end. He repeated this movement several times.

"What did you fly? Some modern plane?"

"MIGS, MIG-17s!" Vojda said. MIG-17s. They were well known, and they could be talked about. He was glad he was able to redeem himself with the MIG-17.

"I've never even seen a jet from really close up," said Havránek disappointedly. It seemed to him that this was not fair at all. He liked airplanes, and Vojda was much younger. He could have been his son. "It all changes so quickly, and the years run away with you."

"Changes?" Jarda flapped the edge of his tunic in an attempt at a joke. "I wouldn't even say it changes. Same old fashion. Same cut . . ." He realized he had interrupted Pilot and he fell silent in mid-sentence. They were all silent for a moment, and then they smiled at one another in sudden relaxation. It was a joke after all.

"I don't know them. We must have a session together some day, when there's more time." The time had revived in Pilot when he was young and had got more from women than mere letters. An

enthusiasm for adventures, an anabasis and a faith which he fulfilled in the end. Long night-flights over Germany aboard unwieldy
Wellingtons. Conversion training to fighters and the feeling of
screaming speed on patrols over the sea. Mosquitoes chasing a V-1.
Then all this within him turned against Vojda. Of course, Vojda
was not one of those who proclaimed they had discovered the truth.
He had still been too young when everything Pilot believed in and
everything that meant anything to him had turned into nothing.
But Vojda was obviously satisfied with it all. MIG-17s.

"There's no more time today. It'll be roll call in a minute. But
come along, come along any time!" And when Vojda again began
to sink into uncertainty, he asked him suddenly and without any
transition how long his sentence was. A question that could be
asked *here* without any transition. It belonged to the basic concepts
of local social conversation. It even preceded questions about
health and family.

"A year and a half," said Vojda. "Eighteen meters. I killed
someone, and I had a few drinks inside me." ("Meters" was the
camp slang for "months.")

"That's not all that much." With a little bitter humor, Havránek thought of the irreplaceable part of his life that had flowed
away in prison. Without his having killed anyone. He spoke with
the voice of a calm and thoughtful man burning disturbing letters
from beautiful, disturbingly beautiful, women immediately after
reading them. It was at the same time the voice of a girl who gives
a false telephone number to an importuner she cannot shake off. He
turned toward the window. Günther, the angular, elegant German,
was just crossing the yard in the direction of the workshop huts. He
had slippers on his feet and held his boots in his hand. He was
speaking to someone standing right under the window, who could
not be seen. He opened his mouth, raised his hand, and dropped one
of the boots. He shouted something unintelligible and pointed to
the door of the shoemaker's workshop. Günther was inside for an

attempt to cross the border, and he was due to go home in a few days. Exceptionality, envy, pity. A handful of vague feelings. By coincidence, the border guard who had detained Günther and had later been imprisoned for something unconnected with Günther was also in the camp. They were on good terms with one another, just as the prosecutor imprisoned for accepting bribes was on good terms with the prisoners he had once prosecuted. They knew one another, and they were not strange to one another in this generally hostile environment. In this world of misunderstanding.

"I don't know," said Vojda. "I really wouldn't like to disturb you, but I don't know anyone here. . . ." Before he could finish his sentence and before Pilot or Jarda could reply, the loud-speaker rang out in the corridor, hoarsely announcing the Knight's roll-call parade.

"There's no question of disturbing us," said Jarda. "This is the atelier, you understand, and if they found you here, there'd be a stink." He banged the lids onto the paint cans. He closed the yellow and the red. He took the pencil stump from the blue and wiped the paint from it on the edge of the can. Only authorized persons, of course, could be in the atelier, and this *could,* of course, lead to a row, but Vojda could just as well be an authorized person if Jarda really wanted it. But he did not want it.

Around the hut sounded the bawling of the prisoner orderlies, the shuffling steps of many feet, a timid hum. And it was slowly dying away.

"Come on," Pilot said to them. "The Knight's on duty, we can't stay here." The Knight knew no pardon. All the posters in the world were not important enough for him. In addition, he had certain difficulties in counting, and he always wanted to have the prisoners en masse and drawn up in fives.

Then the loud-speaker rang out again:

"I warn all prisoners that they must have leather boots and leggings on parade!" And when the crowd began to pour back indoors, he ordered: "I repeat, everyone must have leather boots and leggings!"

Leggings had only found their way into the prisoners' equipment the past winter, when the army had withdrawn them from service once and for all. Drumstick, as one of the guards was nicknamed, had introduced them with the words: "You were always complaining you were cold. Well, now you're getting leggings." Soon it was also revealed that leggings could be an important, another important, item in the process of re-education. The wearing of them began to be demanded always and everywhere, if gum boots were not being worn. Miners at the damp coal faces and the men on the construction site sometimes got gum boots. Today, the Knight had had the bright idea of perfecting the parade with his order about leather boots. Of course, you could not tuck your trousers into boots. Wearing leggings, for the purpose of re-education and correction, the duty of displaying leather boots, the addition to the preceding order. Something absolutely unnecessary and humiliating in its unnecessariness.

A hut orderly opened the door of the atelier without knocking.

"Can't you hear? It's parade. Get along!"

The orderly was probably a little impatient, perhaps also somewhat full of his position. Pilot, of course, said nothing. He was fastening his boot and was completely wrapped up in doing this (having your boots in the atelier shielded you from the evening inspection for cleanliness). But Jarda buttoned up his jacket and felt he had had just about enough.

"Go to hell!" he said.

roll call

The white and naked body, spreading with no shame,
exposes to the bed
its fateful splendor and hidden pride
of beauty given it by Nature.

—Charles Baudelaire

Hot call

they formed up in fives as always, quite willingly, even if their willingness was also a recognition of necessity. They came to terms with it as a matter of routine. Forming up, roll call—that was necessity. They came to terms with it, and they were satisfied if it did not last too long. Perhaps just as we silently forgive women all the love affairs experienced without us, so long as they are hidden behind the words: *It was nothing. It meant nothing to me.*

Whatever inward feelings they may have had, they went out freely and willingly at a mere call from the loud-speaker. There was no greater summons than the hysterical bawling of the orderlies and brigade leaders provoked by the Knight's announcement. If the guards happened to find a missing prisoner in one of the huts, the orderly responsible was sent to suffer with him in the bunker. And so, for the most part, everything went as smoothly as a puppet show. The shifts were drawn up according to the gaps in the concrete in one way or another, the orderlies shrieked in the huts, and the guards from the Knight's shift stood at their posts, with their hands behind their backs. In these hands, most of them held truncheons. Some of them had them hanging on straps from their wrists. Some of them had them on their belts. Bobo had none. Bobo did not give a damn about his career.

In front of hut six, the home of Havránek, Jarda, Vojda, and the whole of their shift, stood Drumstick. There was always one guard or another there when there was a parade on. In the Knight's shift, it was Drumstick, who was also education officer and the author of most of the slogans. He regarded himself as the discoverer of Jarda and had all the pride of a Maecenas who has *made* someone. Jarda and the posters were his pride and joy (he had also received for it a special bonus from the commandant, as a reward for exemplary work). He would usually pass the time until the beginning of the roll call by searching among the clothes and socks hung from the bars of the ground-floor windows. He was looking for illegal food, or at least empty food jars. The prisoners used them for drinking coffee and tea when they had any, and drinking led to the formation of cliques, to discussions, and to undesirable, non-re-educative friendships and gatherings. Because of this, the guards smashed them—perhaps there was some other reason, too, perhaps even an internal directive from the commandant himself, an order for the breaking of glasses. But today there were only gherkin bottles full of milk behind the windows. It was the fifth of the month. On the fifth, the fifteenth, and the twenty-fifth, miners who had fulfilled the norm were issued half a quart of milk.

Between the hut and the concrete strip was a strip of mud several yards wide. The prisoners, in a vain attempt to keep their boots clean, tried to jump over it on loose bricks and broken pieces of planking. (Dirty boots could get you into trouble.) Drumstick watched them indifferently. The jailers wanted to do a big spring-cleaning in their common room today, and they needed to select someone in the course of the parade. Someone with an unbuttoned jacket, with dirty shoes or—a very good idea those leggings—someone without leggings. Drumstick was small and sickly. Roll call was the high point of his life. Today it could no longer be said what kind of man he had been originally or had wanted to be. His job as a guard had marked him for life. He knew that the prisoners laughed at him and thought little of him. Not even his power could force them to acknowledge him. But at parades, he was a cog in a working mechanism; he had seventeen hundred prisoners. He liked himself in this role.

Günther, the strange German who knew no German, stood at the very end. He was poking a matchstick in the corner of his mouth, and he was still carefully groomed down to the careful wave in his hair. Only, for this parade, he had put his cap on. With due caution, so as not to spoil his hair. He had his boots at the shoemaker's and did not think of them. He was aware that he was going home in a few days, but he did not reflect on it. He did not in fact think of anything at all, despite the fact that, two rows in front of him, dressed in equally sour prison gray, stood his captor, the former border guard. Whenever they met now, they smiled at one another. They had long ago said everything to one another that they needed to say. The border guard had in any case been Günther's salvation. He had caught him while he was cutting through the first belt of wire. The next line of wire in that fantastic border strip, which in fact made the whole country into one great camp, was electrified. A mere trifle, five thousand volts and a sizable number of amperes designed to turn a man into a mere black cinder.

The crowds slowly leveled out. The trickle of prisoners jumping over the mud had died away, and the brigade leader was just straightening up the last incomplete row of five—Günther's—when an orderly with a dirty red band on his sleeve came out of the hut. He hesitated in front of the mud, with its protruding islands of brick. Then he saw the brigade leader, raised his hand and called to him: "Still three to come!" He took a jump and landed on the nearest brick.

Right after this, first Vojda, then Jarda and Havránek emerged from the entrance grille. The last summons had been issued, and the Knight and his counting squad were already marching out from the gate and making for the first file of the first shift. The chairman of the camp's self-administration (the former prosecutor sentenced for corruption and placed in this prisoner's backwater in safe anticipation of parole, because there would certainly be no doubt about the effects of re-education in his case) was just making his report.

Drumstick raised his head and shouted reproachfully in the direction of Pilot and Jarda: "You damn fools, what the hell do you think you're doing!"

And the brigade leader waiting at the end of the ranks of his shift just said: "Where are you, men?" Because it was Pilot and Jarda. For Vojda's benefit, he added: "Vojda, man, for God's sake, you're getting lazy early."

The trio came slowly up to him and filled in the spaces in the file. Günther, the strange German who had never learned German because he had always lived in Czechoslovakia; behind him Hercog, the scrap-iron dealer from Bratislava, with five years of Auschwitz and six years of the uranium mines at Jáchymov in his past, who greeted them with the words: "Well, fine ones you are, coming late when the Knight's on duty." With his age, his experience, and everything that, in the camp environment, counted as a human asset, a quality, a sign of hardness and toughness, with all that Hercog should in fact have belonged to the aristocracy of the camp, but he did not. He had been in Auschwitz because he was a Jew, and there had remained in him for all time too much fear, too little will to take things to extremes. He believed in small certainties rather than great aims. He was satisfied with the small things of life. The lower bunk, which could be made more easily and on which you could stretch out more easily in the daytime as well. Occasionally, he spoke in tones of downtroddenness, of eternal self-pity and complaint about the unkindness of fate. Now he turned to Havránek and said: "I'm surprised at you, you of all people, such an old jailbird. . . ." Being an old jailbird predestined you to the possession of certain qualities, just as a woman is predestined by the measure of her charm.

The roll call dragged on slowly, like all roll calls taken by the Knight. He was in no hurry today either—those difficulties with counting! He walked slowly around the first rank and fished out anyone without the prescribed leather boots and leggings. Despite his difficulties with arithmetic, he did his job efficiently and calmly. Drumstick, too, jumped carefully across the mud and began to walk up and down behind the back of the files. Here and there, there was a small knot of people, as prisoners without leggings and wearing high boots tried to find a place where their feet could not be seen. Not even the devil could have guessed what the Knight had dreamed up this time. The Knight had started it, and it was clear that the other shift commanders would imitate him in order not to give the impression of trying to shirk their duty and their mission in life, their service to society and the working class.

The shadow of the hut fell on Pilot's shift. At five in the afternoon in April, the sun does not stand too high in the sky. Opposite, still in its light, the prisoners without boots and leggings stood by the wall of the bunker. They all stood out twice as much, just like the obvious unpleasantness of the punishment that awaited them for ignoring the shift commander's order—"I said leggings and leather boots!"

Hercog changed places with Günther. Jarda looked at the sunlight over by the bunker and said to Pilot behind him: "It's nice, we've got the worst behind us now. Now it'll fly and rush along!" He meant the worst part of the year. Summer passed more quickly in the camp than winter, and it was also less unpleasant.

For Vojda, this "full-scale" parade was again something new.

Hercog turned his head to Günther (the feeling of fear and of discipline from which it derived did not allow him to turn all the way around).

"Go and change your shoes, Günther!"

Günther shrugged his shoulders.

"Fuck that, Mr. Hercog. My boots are at the shoemaker's." Although Günther, the Sudeten German, did not know any German, he had inherited feelings of anti-Semitism, and Hercog looked like a Jew boy straight out of the cartoons in the Goebbels press.

"Günther, go on! I've got some spare boots by my bed!" Hercog was incensed by disrespect for a given order, as he was by Günther's indifference to the danger he sensed was coming. It was necessary to be lost in the crowd, inconspicuous, a nobody, a nothing. Less than a nothing. He had lived the life of a dog for too long to be able to understand that the opposite was equally true.

But Jarda, too, looked at Günther's feet.

"You're really going to get it in the neck!"

"Günther, you know what they're like! Why the hell are they interested in the shoemaker!"

The Knight was now counting the shift standing at right angles to theirs. When he had finished—and that could be in three or four minutes—he would come over to them. Hercog was still trying to persuade Günther. But Drumstick was already standing behind them. He ran his eyes over Pilot's, Jarda's, Vojda's, Günther's, and Hercog's feet. He spotted the gum boots and took a second look at them to make certain. They did him good. A catch! A man for spring-cleaning in the common room. He smiled like a man who has finally reached maturity.

"How is it you've got gum boots on?" he said sweetly, and when Günther looked around uncertainly, he thundered: *"Yes, you!* Don't gape, go and stand by the bunker!"

"I . . ." said Günther.

"Sir." Hercog spoke up—he, too, was one of the few prisoners whose number went right back to the beginnings of the camp, but, nonetheless, he had had to summon up all his courage before opening his mouth. "His boots really are at the shoemaker's."

"You keep quiet, Hercog!" Drumstick nodded his head toward

the bunker and touched Günther's elbow. "Go and stand by the bunker! How many times do I have to tell you!" He displayed the calm decisiveness of a self-assured man.

"My boots are at the shoemaker's," Günther replied without turning around. He was, after all, on parade and they had been ordered to stand at attention. "And I'll be going home in twenty days."

The last remark really enraged Drumstick. He shrieked hysterically: "Even if you were being discharged in an hour, you'll still appear on parade properly equipped, understand?" He took a step forward and mingled with the prisoners. He pushed Günther from behind. As he spread his fingers on Günther's jacket, you could see clearly stretched out the top joints with the hammerlike nails that had earned him his nickname. They looked like little hammers or drumsticks. *"Get a move on!"* And then, when he found himself unable to move Günther from the spot: *"What's your name?"*

"Tomschin," said Günther. "31 67."

Drumstick took out a notebook and wrote down the name and number. He blew out a breath.

"Tomschin? Well, off you go, Tomschin, your place is by the bunker."

It seemed that Drumstick had regained his lost calm by writing the name down in his notebook. He thrust the pad into the breast pocket of his tunic, fastened the button, and fixed his ball-point pen to the edge of his pocket by its clip.

Even now, Günther did not turn around.

"I won't go anywhere." He gulped and added less obstinately: "I was unable to bring my boots. They're at the shoemaker's."

This was too much for Drumstick. He was like an ardent lover who spends half a year looking for proof of suspected unfaithfulness and eventually finds it. He throws it triumphantly into his beloved's face and gets the indifferent reply: *So what?*

"Did you hear my order? *Fall out!*" he shouted and clenched his fists in front of his chest. He was a head, perhaps one and a half heads, smaller than the German. And Günther, for the two years of his sentence, had been working as a breaker at the coal face. He was built for the job. Even before this, he had done only hard physical work.

"I won't go," he said softly. He sensed that they had passed the point of no return. As far as the boots were concerned, he was in the right. Failure to obey an order was on another level. It was not the sort of thing that was redeemed by spring-cleaning. They were no longer talking about his boots, the torn sole that had formed a shark's jaw and Fousek's warning: *Get that mended, man!* It had all somehow gone beyond the bounds of a thing that could still be explained and understood. He scraped his feet on the spot. . . . In twenty days . . .

Drumstick rushed out far beyond the rank, so that the Knight could see him, and yelled:

"Shift commander! Shift commander!"

Pilot put his hand on Günther's shoulder.

"Go on, you damned fool!"

"Go on!" repeated several scattered and hidden voices.

Günther scraped his feet again. To hell, he thought to himself. After all, my boots really are at the shoemaker's. Such idiocy. All these jailers are out of their minds. Then he walked around Hercog and stepped out in front of the shift. Slowly—as slowly as he could —he walked to the sunlight by the bunker. To the brightly illumi- nated knot of men standing there. Callow youth of twenty-two years, he had not yet got used to the fact that you always lose in situations like this.

As soon as the Knight heard Drumstick's martial bellowing, he looked around for the voice. He ran a few steps on his grotesque feet, holding in his hand the notebook in which he had been writing down the strength of the individual shifts for the final reckoning. He spotted Drumstick and yelled: "What is it?"

By this time, Günther was marching across the yard. His gum boots formed long, moving folds over the toes. Drumstick pointed his hand at him, with its deformed fingers.

"He is unwilling to fall out. *He refused to obey an order!*" His long period of service had left its mark on him. The guards expressed themselves in legal concepts picked up from court verdicts. These were irritating concepts: *He is unwilling. He refused!*

The Knight broke into a run. He seemed to be carried along by some wave.

"*Who?*"

Drumstick again pointed at Günther.

"That one!"

The Knight's canter had lost its justification now that the rebel had come to reason and fallen out. But insubordination, *insubordination, he refused, he is unwilling*—all this aroused the Knight's wrath. Insubordination had the same effect on him as the color red on bulls and turkeys. Perhaps so as not to appear ridiculous, perhaps because Günther really was walking quite slowly, but most likely without any reason at all, simply because he was moving, the Knight did something he would regret. A moment before, he had again got mixed up in his counting—156 plus 561 equals 611—and had stumbled in front of the brigade leader of the neighboring shift. And this disturbance meant starting all over again. He ran up to Günther and seized him by the collar with the full force of his two hundred and fifty pounds and shoved him forward. There was no personal hatred in this. Chiefly just the knowledge that the man in front of him was only a prisoner, that he could give his anger free rein. A small deficiency of internal correctives and external inhibitions. He had come down from behind on Günther, who was by now almost at the bunker, and attacked him without warning. The German, in fact, had to take a few faster steps, but then he stopped dead. He worked at the coal face, and he could load a ton of coal with his spade in twenty minutes. Sometimes, quite often in fact, a rail would yield under the weight of the loaded truck. The coupling would break, the wagon would be derailed, and it would have to be put back on the track again while it was still loaded. Günther did this, too. He had the greatest strength of the whole gang. Now he stopped as though about to lift a derailed truck up on his back. This time, there was no Pilot standing behind him to say: Don't do it. Nor was it certain whether Pilot would still have given this advice at this moment.

The Knight slackened his grip on Günther's collar and blushed. Günther knew how he should stand. He saw how he was to stand and did not yield. By now, the eyes of half the camp were on him. The murmur in the ranks died away, and even the guards stood rooted to the spot in expectation. The Knight blushed deeply, the veins in his neck stood out, and then he turned blue in the face. Someone in the crowd shouted: "Now you've lost count!"

The Knight knew that this was directed at him, and that once again he looked ridiculous. He was not strong enough to move Günther from the spot. He let go of his collar and breathed hard.

"And get your cap off!" He struck the prisoner across the head. Günther's cap fell to the ground.

"Pick it up!"

Günther looked the Knight in the eyes and then bent down. He could have hit back much more and much harder than the Knight, but he controlled himself. He knew how incidents of that sort ended. The number twenty came into his head. In twenty days, the Knight's power ended. There would be other Knights, of course, but not this one. He picked up the cap and started straightening up.

Then the Knight kneed him, and Günther fell over.

Günther stood up and tried to walk away, but the Knight held him back. The tension, the silence, and the expectation had been broken by the blows. Guards converged on them from all sides, and whistling, jeering, and shouting spread from shift to shift.

Seventeen hundred men lived in the camp, perhaps even ten or so more. For the moment, it was the roar of a waterfall. The sound of a packed stadium when the home team scores a goal a minute before the end of the game in a completely hopeless situation. It was something like scoring a goal. Moments of struggle which we remember. We want to roar like this so often, but we rarely have the opportunity. Because of wives presumed or known to be in another man's arms. Because of girls who have realized that other men are just as good for making love as we are. Because of the hopelessness of desire in stuffy dormitories full of quarrels over whether to open or close the windows, full of human smell, dust, and despair. Because of the homosexuals conversing lovingly, and the energy lost in masturbation.

Günther heard this roaring, and so did the Knight. He knew at whom it was directed. He stood up and banged the dust out of his cap on his knee. The mud deposited on the concrete strip turned in time into a layer of dust that could only be washed off by a thorough downpour. It had not rained yet this year, and the remains of the ashes put down in the winter also remained on the concrete. He looked the Knight straight in the face.

It seemed to the Knight that the ranks of prisoners had moved toward him. The muscles stood out on his neck, and he blushed again in his attempts to calm down. He pushed Günther again by the shoulder and bellowed: "Go on! Go on!"

Drumstick, Coathanger, Bobo, Death's-head, and Batista ran up. The whole of the Knight's shift in the camp, apart from the men on the machine-gun towers and the reserves in the guardhouse at the gate.

"Don't shove me around . . ." said Günther, but by now someone had clipped handcuffs around his right wrist, and then he felt many hands forcing his hands together behind his back so that they could pinion them. He did not try to resist. He had understood the uselessness of resistance the moment the Knight had hit him. I've got my boots at the shoemaker's, he had wanted to say. But he knew that all words were superfluous. The handcuffs had clicked onto his left hand, too, and he was dragged toward the gate amid a knot of jailers. He felt a little regret about this day that had begun so very normally. In twenty days. Something like a rebuke to the world. Fear. After all, they were all shouting, and he would go to the bunker alone. He was not prepared for it. He would be cold and hungry. Twenty days—but what if they used him as a warning, a discouragement to all the others? How far off would the twenty days then be?

The Knight began to feel even more uncertain. The absence of the guards behind the brigades (they were all taking a hand in dragging Günther to the gate) caused the roar to grow louder. Unless, of course, he lashed out at the prisoners, but not in front of so many witnesses. It could not be said that the Knight was afraid. No, there was no question of his being afraid. But not being in control of the camp meant getting into trouble. And he was clearly not in control of something here. Because of this parade, dinner would be delayed, and tomorrow someone might refuse to work on the grounds that he had not had enough to eat today. The plan. The commandant. The daily program. A cross on his black card.

"Stop it! Stop it!" But in the din that was going on all around, he could hardly hear his own voice. *"Dismiss to huts!"* (Instruction 1. In emergencies, lock the prisoners into the huts and guard the area outside them with firearms and dogs.) An emergency, just my luck. *"Dismiss to huts!"* He was alone. All the guards were dragging Günther to the gate. They could not get through the turnstile. He turned around to see what they were doing. Hurry up, he thought. He left-turned and took two or three rapid steps. The roar grew even louder:

There he goes, the bastard.

I can't run away, he was saying to himself. Calmness creates an impression. But he knew that he *was* running away, and those seventeen hundred roaring prisoners knew it, too. *Hurry up*—and then he really did start running. The camp was without guards. Seventeen hundred men stood in the middle of the yard between the huts and roared. They stayed put. They were waiting. They felt almost satisfied. Many of them found it funny.

After a moment, the camp loud-speakers sounded. First, like a sort of undertone in the general roar, but as the noise died down it gradually became intelligible. The loud-speakers. This was something totally different from the helpless Knight running about and shouting in the middle of the camp. They were accustomed to obeying the loud-speakers. The loud-speakers ordered dismissal and gave a warning that the dogs would be let into the camp in three minutes.

A knot of guards emerged from the gate and broke into a run with outstretched hands in which they brandished their truncheons against the ranks.

"Dismiss, dismiss!"

The main gate was opened, and the dog-handlers came inside with their animals. The Alsatians could not get through the turnstile. Glovelet carried a machine gun out of the guardhouse and set it up by the fence strip beside the gate. He lay down behind it and took his grip. The shooting holes above the floor of the towers also opened and bristled with gun barrels with perforated silencers.

The first ranks began to thin out as soon as the loud-speakers rang out. All at once the narrow hut doors were full of men they could not accommodate. Behind the backs of the increasingly desperate crush, the guards with the dogs advanced slowly.

It had happened recently, in the autumn, that a drunken guard had fired from one of the towers into a chance grouping of prisoners. On another occasion, during one of the desperate and stupid attempts to escape, attempts without even a 1 per cent chance of success, a prisoner sleeping peacefully in bed in his hut had been hit by a shot. *Force majeure*. They had also shot a prisoner who had been playing with a kitten at the edge of the fence strip on the last day of his sentence. The kitten had run into the area strewn with white sand and had brought instant death to him, even though he had only stretched one hand into the prohibited area. The guards in the towers were rewarded when they shot well. It was a sign that they were doing their job conscientiously. Everyone knew of some such case. Everyone had heard of one. They stopped shouting and pushed wildly into the narrow doors of the huts. No one had any desire to become the melancholy hero of another such story, even if the odds were only seventeen hundred to one or seventeen hundred to two.

"Christ, now it's really beginning," said Vojda, when he was at last standing in the middle of the dormitory again. It was the brigade leader's room, the only one where they had had a free bed for him yesterday. He was not speaking to anyone in particular. It was just a sentence cast into the air, a comment on the situation of a man spending his first day in the camp. A man who had had his arm broken by the crowd in the crush at the entrance was moaning in the corner. Vojda had been perhaps only one step behind him when it happened, even though there were at least seven men crushed in between them, but he had seen the man wedge his elbow into the bars, struggle in vain for a moment, attempt to resist and free himself, and he had also heard the snap and the roar of pain as the bone broke.

"You get used to it, chum," Jarda said, a little ironically. He was spreading dripping on a slice of bread. Pilot was cutting his bread in silence. It was gloomy in the dormitory. A group of people had crowded at the windows in the hope even now of seeing something out of the ordinary outside. Drumstick went past, shrieked some order or threat at them, and the window area was rapidly vacated. The brigade leader was trying to negotiate some help for the man with the broken arm at the closed grille, but the guard merely shrugged his shoulders. The shift commander had ordered the huts to be locked. Then they saw Günther walking in handcuffs between two guards on his way to the bunker.

"Well, I told him so," said Hercog with all the reproachfulness of a man who has been insufficiently believed, and he shuffled off to lie down on the bed he had won over the years in the corner by the stove. If the grilles were locked with chains, you could safely lie down even in the daytime. The clanking when they were unlocked was loud enough to give a timely warning.

Vojda looked at Jarda's dripping. It reminded him of the sausage in Dobrovský's parcel, which was still on the minds of everyone here. Dobrovský, too, was from the brigade leader's dormitory.

Dripping was a valuable commodity in the camp and a form of payment that was always acceptable. With a little dripping, a man could fill himself up and make a decent meal of it even when it was one of the variations on beans, peas, lentils, and similar delicacies, which formed the staple part of the camp menu. Not being dependent in your hunger on the cookhouse was also one of the fundamental feelings of freedom and independence.

Jarda spotted Vojda's look. He remembered his own first days in the camp and stopped thinking about the sausage and the three little green gherkins. He remembered the prisoner who had in those days given him half his own ration of bread. *In those days,* in those days. Almost as much as Jarda's stomach and frame of mind had needed. He held out the dripping to Vojda and said: "Do you want to spread some for yourself?"

He did not ask Pilot, even though their supplies were shared. As far as food was concerned, Pilot was most interested in the supply line from the pit. He looked on food very much as he looked on women. He liked them, but he was able to put them out of his mind when he did not need them. And he was happy not so much for the very fact of their existence, but for everything that came his way through them.

Vojda nodded. He had spent three weeks in prison on basic rations. There were too many differences in quality and quantity between the diet of a pilot in the service and what he had eaten for the last three weeks for him to be able to refuse. The dripping with its dots left over from frying was like a mirage. Jarda also lent him his knife, a huge gardener's chopper, smuggled, like the dripping, from the mine. When Vojda thanked him, he merely waved his hand in the air. As a small boy, he had dreamed of becoming a pilot. Perhaps this was why Havránek ended up beside him here in later life. And Vojda knew a piece of the same sky.

They chewed in silence for a long while. Pilot smoked and gazed into space. Perhaps he was thinking of the beautiful woman who was just writing him a letter, one of his letters. The huts were still locked up, and the guard dogs stalked the yard on their handlers' leashes. Normally, they would be having dinner at this time.

Vojda was immersed in the confusion. The bread and dripping had brought him closer to the others, and he felt obliged to say something. Günther's fate had aroused him, even though it was part and parcel of what he had always thought about prisons. What everyone always thought about them, both he and they, the fighter boys, the pilots first-class. He pointed outside to where they had been standing shortly before and said: "I didn't know that *this* was allowed." He had in his voice the amazement of a boy scout who has just discovered that people tell lies even though they should not.

Jarda waved his hand with the knife. He did not chew the bread because, at some time, he had lost his front teeth. He cut it into cubes, as old people do.

"They're all lousy Bolsheviks." By this, he meant not only the Knight, but all the people he knew, all the people his father had included when he used to say: "You see, Jarda, before, I used to have this machine, Bedřich, and you to feed. Now I've got all that gang in the office on my back." Bedřich was Jarda's brother, and the machine was an old Tatra car, which rather had them to feed, because Jarda's father drove it as a taxi driver. Under the heading of "lousy," he also included the woman caretaker of the house where they lived, the spy of the people's administration, who had once written in her assessment and report on reputation that his family did not adorn the windows on festive occasions and did not take part in demonstrations. This had played a not-exactly-unsubstantial role in forming Jarda's life. He was not accepted for secondary school. His father a former self-employed taxi driver; the nonadornment of the windows—this afforded no guarantee of a positive attitude to the socialist system, et cetera. He was glad that he could describe the direction in which he had then gone as the work of someone else. As something which had overtaken him and borne down on him. Being in the right is a good feeling.

His words, of course, rather surprised Vojda. He was a member of the Party. All the fighter boys, pilots first-class, were in the Party. To be a fighter pilot and not a Party member was simply unthinkable. It was just as necessary a prerequisite as good health, something so normal that he never thought twice about it. He had the impression that things would not work out any other way. Many other people in the camp had carried Party cards before they came here, but it had not been the very foundation of their lives, as it had been for Vojda. Since his youth at the military school—and this was not something dead and gone but recent and still relatively fresh in his memory—he had seen his membership in the Party as an indestructible furrow, as a belief that from this year's grain would come next year's ear of corn. A guarantee. So many splendid models of humanity were, after all, Communists. The boys. The heroes of the Resistance. Perhaps somewhere there were some dark spots, but that was really none of his business. Pilot, too, of course, had been a Resistance hero, an airman in England. There was something inexplicable here, but the idea was good and it could not be scorned. But he found Jarda sympathetic as well, and the bread and dripping which he liked so much had come from Jarda.

"When someone's a shit . . ." He did not know what he actually meant. That everywhere there is someone who is a shit and someone who is good. It suddenly struck him as too shallow. Too banal. "If the people in the Party knew what— The Knight wouldn't be here much longer."

Jarda began to laugh and almost choked. He swallowed with exhaustion. It cost him a lot of effort. The sweat stood out on his brow.

"Well, yes, you see," he said. "You've stepped straight out of the pages of some textbook, haven't you?" He addressed himself to Pilot, nodding his head toward Vojda. "Is it really possible? Who are you trying to fool, Mr. Officer? This is a camp we're in, and we don't live on goulash speeches here, you know."

"Poor Günther," said old Hercog from his corner. "They're taking it out of him now, but I told him to go and change his boots."

"There are human beings in the Party." Vojda felt like a man who has done something improper in public and has been noticed by everyone. The incident at the gate, the sausage, the uniform he had arrived in. "Perhaps the Knight doesn't belong to the Party at all." He was slowly beginning to understand that this dormitory and a place like the camp were not the most suitable surroundings for a conversation of this sort and for the development of Marxist-Leninist ideas. But at the same time he felt that he was in this way passing beyond the bounds of his greenness among all these men who had seen more, experienced more, remembered more and, it seemed, could also do more than he could. Apart from the feeling of a man who flies planes. Apart from the fact that he had been nearest of them in time to a woman. He cast around for some firm ground before they began to shout and curse. But he sensed the uncertainty of the ground he stood on as against the firm reality of all else. "In our unit . . ." The unit had been his home. In many ways it had been even more than a home. It was the only place to which he could return, had to return, and wanted to return.

". . . you are all worth a load of shit." Jarda completed the sentence for him. "Is it possible? Is it possible?" He shook his head in incomprehension. "Go and tell the Knight all about your unit. He's one of you, from this Party of yours, you're in the same boat, aren't you?" His calm and astonishment had abandoned him. Drops of saliva flew from his mouth.

"Perhaps he isn't in the Party at all," Vojda objected again, but he knew that was probably not the case. Pilots first-class and prison guards differed in color of uniform and rate of pay. Not in the cut of their uniforms. And not in the general conditions attached to their work.

"He is in the Party," Pilot pronounced. "Last week I had to clean up his club room. There was a list of candidates for the committee for this year hanging up there. His name was on it."

"They're a gang of tramps," Jarda burst out again.

Someone rebuked them nervously.

"Forget it!" The debate was now moving in areas where it was ceasing to be just an exchange of views. For Jarda, it could mean the bunker, if not some idiotic trial, and for Vojda—being crushed by a truck somewhere down the mine.

"The Party can't answer for every idiot!" Vojda threw up his hands and let them fall. He had not wanted a quarrel. He sensed he was losing, even though what he was defending was not so much himself as the group at the airfield, well-fed, contented pilots first-class, their games of volleyball and their bathing in the Elbe. He sensed he was losing, within himself and against the others. They were like receivers with a wave length on which he could not transmit. "Well, can it?"

"Whoever has the power has the responsibility, too. And if he doesn't want the responsibility, he shouldn't have the power," said Pilot. "But this—" he pointed somewhere over his shoulder in a gesture that took in the yard, the camp, the Knight, Günther, and the feelings of all present—"this is only a little piece of the system." He waved his hand and looked around him. "It wouldn't be bad to have a go at the Knight." Here spoke the man who had not hesitated at the right time to tell the whole parole board, with the exception of the secretary, to go to the end of his alimentary canal. He had principles and a sense of moderation in all things. Justice. Fair play. And the spirit of the age. The Günther affair was between them. He was ready to intervene. And this was a matter that demanded intervention, according to his taste.

"As a Party member . . ."

Pilot waved his hand again, distastefully and imperiously.

"A shit." He did not mince words. "You can go and stuff yourself with that here. Try and talk to the Knight as a Party member."

"I've got it in my blood," said Vojda. He struck himself as a hero in a film, and he felt satisfied. Faith can be not only the result of a rational process but equally well the result of a softened brain. Pilot's look cut him down. Flying, volleyball, bathing in the Elbe— this, after all, was something quite different. This was what made their group into a group, and not the infinitely boring encounters with boring problems.

"All right," he then heard Pilot say. "If you've got it in you, just leave it inside and don't parade around here like a circus horse. We don't play at religion here. We've all been confirmed." Pilot scratched his upper lip with a matchstick. "It could be done. What they'd do would interest me."

Jarda watched him uncomprehendingly. He was not quite clear what Pilot was talking about. In fact, the whole dormitory was watching him.

"To go to *them,* you understand. As witnesses. So they'd let Günther go." Havránek laughed. "A sign of re-education. Consistent reading of the laws . . . Do you think he doesn't know what a stupidity he committed when he laid into him publicly? You *can't* go around beating people up, after all, can you? After all, our police don't use *force*—that's a method the Party has put a stop to. Don't you read the papers?"

"You can't go around beating people up—you can't go around beating people up," someone announced ironically. "It's all stupidity."

They looked around for the voice. It was an elderly prisoner. He was known to be inside for black-market dealings with apartments. He clearly regretted already that he had let himself be provoked, that he had spoken out and drawn attention to himself. But he was not going to yield.

"It's stupidity," he said again. "Just prove that they're going around beating up anyone at all. They were only defending themselves. Günther attacked them, didn't he?" Yes, it was always like that. That was how it was always described in the verdicts of the court.

"Didn't you see it?" asked Pilot.

"What?"

"The Günther business." Havránek was a little impatient.

"Yes, I saw it," said the man.

"Well, how about going to testify?"

The man climbed onto his bed. He disappeared into it. He stretched out.

"Well, I'll say I saw nothing, understand?" He paused and looked to see what impression he had made. And also to find some way of justifying himself. "I've got twenty months behind me, and I want to go home, do you understand?" He had twenty months behind him and sixteen ahead of him. Parole.

"Perhaps you will," said Pilot. "We've all got something behind us and something in front of us." He laughed. "And Günther's only got twenty days."

"I don't give a damn about your Günther, even if he only has two days to do. He's a Kraut." The man had at last found a cause. A Kraut. Not a fear, but realization. A Kraut. "What does a man like him want . . ." The man was breaking into familiar patterns. SS, OCCUPATION, School prefects in white stockings, Lidice, Heydrich. This was in people, and it aroused the necessary emotions. "To pave Wenceslas Square with our skulls, that's what your Günther wants. . . ." The man was hidden in the gloom of a lower bunk. He yelled: "Am I to bring them down on my head because of him?"

"If a man has stupid arguments, he has to state them at the top of his voice, hasn't he?" Pilot was smiling. He had the man where he wanted him. Havránek had shot down nine German planes during the war. But not everyone had been able to be a fighter pilot. Not everyone had been able to get to England. He did not want to enter into a debate on how necessary or how vital things were. During the time he had been in the camp, Pilot and Günther had probably not even exchanged as much as three words. They had nothing to say to one another. Pilot was quite careful in selecting the people he wanted to say something to.

"Did it help you at your trial that you were against the Germans?" he asked. He naturally knew about the speculation with apartments that had brought the man to the camp. But he did not want to humiliate him on this score.

"I didn't do anything bad. I was helping people."

Yes, of course, Pilot thought to himself, and if you regularly robbed someone here and there in doing so, it was only in the context of these charitable activities. He repeated: "Did it help you that you were against the Germans?"

"No, it didn't help me. . . ." In the man's past, there had been a time, a great time, the greatest time of his life, the revolutionary period, when he had had a machine pistol and the band of the revolutionary guard on his sleeve and had roamed the borderlands with a gang of youths to pacify the Sudeten Germans. They had also engaged in a little stealing in the process. "It didn't help me."

"Then why do you start arguing that Günther's a German? Do you think the Knight would treat you any different?"

"I had my leggings and my leather boots," the man said.

"And why do you start arguing that the Knight's a Party member?" Vojda chipped in.

"Because he is," said Jarda. "And because there's a difference."

"We're living in the twentieth century. . . ." began Vojda.

"Communists in the Middle Ages and the Russians a hundred years before the apes . . ." Jarda interrupted him, but he, too, was prevented from finishing his sentence. There was a clanking from the grille at the entrance. He smirked and stretched his arm out in the direction of the noise: "The twentieth century! Do you hear? The twentieth century, you say?"

An orderly put his head around the door, and at the same time the brigade leader came in.

"Fall in in the corridor!" He looked around. "Where's the man with the broken arm?"

The man with the broken arm was lying down. He had his eyes closed and his face bore the weary expression of a man trying to think of nothing—neither of the pain in his elbow nor of the dispute over Günther. The brigade leader walked over to him.

"Come on, what's your name? I'll take you to sick bay."

The prisoner began to raise himself slowly on his good arm, and Drumstick's bawl rang out in the corridor:

"Well, come along now, men! Fall in! Fall in!" He was remembering his years of military service as an NCO.

"Go and fall down, you shit," someone in the room replied.

They began to get their caps and go out. The brigade leader led the injured man: "While I'm counting, one of the guards will take you to sick bay. He's promised."

Parades were only held in the corridor when there was a heavy frost or for reasons such as today's incident. But far more frequently because of incidents in which the prisoners' patience swelled up and exploded than because of frost. Losing control of the camp was a black mark in the guards' cadre reports. And who wanted to have his cadre report ruined? At best criminal desperadoes or madmen and traitors like that English pilot Havránek, who used to say: "I've got excellent reports, sir, but for another country."

In the corridors, for reasons of space, you had to fall in in close-packed ranks of three. The threes were counted in tens, and then the remainder was added on. An orderly checked over the dormitory. It went relatively quickly, and it was not so uncomfortable as outside. You could not march in the corridor either.

When the strength of the shift had been entered in the Knight's notebook, the brigade leader called them to attention again at the Knight's instructions. The Knight wanted to address them. He loved these moments in which he could explain to the world what sort of man he was and what his intentions had been.

"Men, you know me," he said. *"I warn anyone* who feels like trying something like Tomschin did. You all saw what happened to him. And the same will happen to anyone . . ." New words kept coming into his head as he spoke. "You perhaps know that he was to have gone home in a few days. And you also certainly know how many days are given for what he did!"

Silence. These were the usual words. The same or similar words were used whenever the camp had to fall in in the middle of the night in the yard illuminated by searchlights and was presented with some escapee caught in the attempt. Or with the bullet-riddled and dog-chewed piece of flesh that remained of him. The voice bounced off the walls of the corridor in a dull echo.

Batista took the prisoner with the broken arm by the elbow of his good arm and bent down, or rather stretched down, to the Knight's ear: "I'll take this one to sick bay, all right?"

The Knight gazed into the corridor with its violet-colored light bulbs, stopped speaking for a moment and nodded. Batista disappeared with the injured man.

The Knight straightened up and went on: "When I call you on the loud-speakers, you will go to dinner. You will do so calmly and quietly. One disturbance, and I'll punish the whole shift." It seemed that he felt like wagging his finger at them. "You were going to have a film on Sunday. You won't now! You can thank those who were the first to start shouting outside." He leaned over to the brigade leader and in a whisper, as always, gave him the same orders all over again.

Then, suddenly, a voice rang out in the silence: "Prisoner Havránek, number 12. May I say something, sir?"

The guards at the grille became attentive. The Knight straightened up from the brigade leader's ear and barked: "What do you want? Who is it?"

"Here, sir!"

The Knight walked nervously up to Pilot: "What do you want?"

"Sir, I wanted to ask you to release prisoner Tomschin from the bunker. He hasn't done anything. His boots are at the shoemaker's."

"What?" The Knight was standing about two paces away. He took the two paces, and the veins again stood out on his neck. "What did you say?"

"If he is not released," Havránek continued in a toneless voice, "I am willing to testify for prisoner Tomschin at any time and any place about the manner in which he was treated here."

For a moment, the Knight looked as though he had been struck with a stick. There was a deathly hush. He took his notebook from his pocket: "Name and number!"

Pilot again gave his name and number, and the Knight wrote them down painstakingly. He was breathing heavily. The silence was so complete that it appeared as though he and Pilot were alone in the corridor.

"Is there anyone else asking for Tomschin to be released from the bunker? Anyone else who wants to testify?"

The Knight had years of service in prison camps behind him. But this was the first time something of this sort had come his way. He sometimes heard talk and he sometimes spoke himself of social-ist legality. It was moreover quite a popular subject in these condi-tions. It was also his own beloved legality. He looked at Pilot. They were the same height. He smiled. Pilot was alone. These bourgeois Don Quixotes. This servant of the era that had lost, who would not admit that his time was past.

"Well, *anyone else?*"

If three people asked for anything with only a hint of the cate-gorical about it, it could always be turned, with a bit of skill, into a rebellion by the prisoners. A paragraph of the penal code with the number of years' sentence quoted in two figures at the end.

"No one?"

These good-for-nothings. Thieves. Jailbirds. Cowardly bastards and egoists. Little shopkeepers whom we have deprived of their worm-eaten counters and their bowls of gherkins in muslin. And this particular old bastard who had obviously been given too short a sentence and who thought he could get big just because he had managed to tell the parole board to kiss his ass.

"Anyone else reporting? No one?"

"Sir, prisoner Vojda, 59 77." Vojda was standing right at the very end of the corridor, by the washrooms and toilets. His voice echoed and sounded three times. "I, too, saw how prisoner Tomschin was treated!"

The Knight left Havránek, who was standing stony-faced at attention and yet smiling slightly, and went to take a look at Vojda. The only sound in the silence of the corridor was the squeaking of the Knight's boots. The air-force lieutenant, the former air-force lieutenant, was smaller than the Knight.

"You only arrived yesterday, didn't you?"

"Yes, sir," Vojda looked straight ahead, past the Knight. He, too, had a stony countenance and at the same time a calm, smiling expression.

If dinner had not already been delayed long enough, the Knight would have driven the whole shift out onto the concrete strip and made them march for an hour. Perhaps for two. And made them sing. He would have supervised it all personally. But dinner, just like roll call, was part of the order of the camp. The Knight was not exactly stupid. No one knew the number of crosses, black crosses, in his own cadre reports, apart from those who supplied the material and who had to take care that the number of crosses did not exceed the norm, who had to see to it that their work as counters of black crosses was known. The Knight knew that he could not afford to disturb the routine—and lose control of the camp. Perhaps he was already written off somewhere up above, and a disturbance of the camp routine could break him once and for all. Tomorrow, ten raving madmen like these two would come forward and refuse to work because they had not had enough to eat, and would repeat this to the prosecutor, who hadn't been so friendly lately as he used to be years ago. And it was on the mining work, on the tons of coal extracted, that the guards depended for their

bonuses. The Knight, too. He knew that the pit management was
not particularly fond of him. God only knew what plans they
dreamed up down there where the Knight had never worked.

"You can dismiss!" he said. "Dinner will be in ten minutes."

"Dis-miss!" roared the brigade leader.

The prisoners began to disperse to their dormitories. Pilot was
still standing in position and still smiling slightly. The Knight
walked past as though he did not see him. Issuing orders had
calmed him down a little. He was still master here. He took a step
back toward Havránek: "And you . . ." he said.

"Could the prosecutor please be informed?" The words flowed
from Pilot's lips.

"Don't you worry about it!" shrieked the Knight and walked
out. Glovelet, Drumstick, and Bobo were already waiting for him,
and once he had passed through, they closed the grilles and locked
them.

Pilot went back to the dormitory. In the middle of the corridor,
he met the brigade leader. He was shaking his head.

"I think you're making unnecessary trouble for yourself." They
stood for a moment. "Well, it's your own business."

"It is," said Pilot. "It amuses me, you know."

Someone clapped him on the shoulder: "That was tremen-
dous!" And another clap on the shoulder.

Somehow, of course, he also came across Vojda at the door of
the dormitory.

"After you!" Pilot pointed to the door.

"No, go on." Vojda let him go first. For a moment, they argued
at the door like a couple of Spanish grandees, and had it not been
for the camp loud-speakers ordering their shift to parade for dinner, this would probably have gone on for much longer.

It was not until they were standing in the line outside the cookhouse that Vojda asked: "Do you think he'll call the prosecutor for
you?"

Pilot laughed. "No, I don't really think so." He shook his head.

In every hut hung a copy of the camp regulations and a list of the rights and duties of prisoners. It was their right to have an interview with the prosecutor. A right guaranteed by law.

"But it's his duty, isn't it?"

Pilot laughed again. He was in a good mood, and Vojda was suddenly more comprehensible to him. It struck him that he himself had perhaps once looked like this. A sacred enthusiasm for the one and indivisible justice. Liberty, equality, fraternity.

"Look here, he won't call the prosecutor, but Tomschin—" (he never again called him Günther after this)—"Tomschin must know he's got at least two witnesses in the camp before they're able to trump up some charge against him. *They* . . ." He tossed his head vaguely so as to make clear all that lay hidden behind that *they*. "They know very well they're not in the right. And most of the ones above them know, too, and the ones right at the top as well. But they also want to appear completely honest and just. *They want to.* They know they're not, but they want to, do you get it? They may ignore all sorts of things, but they can't ignore the bare facts in a stink like this. We may win."

The line at the cookhouse window moved forward slowly.

"By the way, we were all pretty decent men in our squadron," said Vojda. He was not so completely convinced about what he was saying. But he wanted Pilot to think that the reality had been such as he described it. Volleyball, swimming in the Elbe, and excursions to the inn had, of course, been a greater bond among them than any Party. But they had all been members of the Party.

"Look, so were we. Wherever there's something going on, there must be a gang of decent men. You can't get pissed without a decent gang."

Meanwhile, the Knight had driven the shift that was to get dinner after them out onto the concrete strip. He was walking alongside the ranks of five and insisting on proper marching.

"You will march until you learn how to do it properly!"

They all knew he was just shouting and acting the fool. He demonstrated the parade march to them and slammed his crooked legs in the high boots against the concrete. "You've got to make a slap like that!" The Knight, too, knew that he was only shouting. When the cookhouse was free, he would have to send them for dinner. Regulations.

But discipline could also be strengthened by means other than marching. There were many known ways of strengthening discipline. There were certainly at least as many as there were ways of loving. If the discipline was in the interests of some higher goal, it could turn into an insuperable and irreconcilable passion. Especially when you had pretty well nothing to do but saunter around the camp with a truncheon in your hand.

This evening, Pilot's shift was exposed to a strengthening of discipline by means of clearing up and putting in order. Order was a wide concept, and it opened the concept to the human mind. The greatest expert on order in the Knight's shift was the guard Death's-head. He was the greatest expert altogether among the guards. Moreover, the Knight's gang in general were considered to be a collection of lousy pigs, apart from Bobo, of course, but he again was an exception.

There was no particular expertise involved. It was enough to have remembered a few tricks from your military service. Dust on the ceiling lamp or the upper edge of the door. Clean soles and dirt around the hobs. Death's-head, of course, had an *attitude* to order. He always went about in a spotless uniform, which looked as though it had just come off a tailor's dummy. Buttons polished and lapels and pockets smooth. He had a pale face with bewitching eyes and a beautiful wife. One of the four women in the camp who wore jailers' uniforms and were employed in the camp administration. So beautiful that she simply *had to* deceive him, because not even a man in a spotless pressed uniform and with eyes like the black huntsman could tie down such a beautiful woman, especially when his appearance betrayed a hint of stomach ulcers and a hint of a defective gall bladder.

It did not take him long to check over the order of the rooms. When they came back from the cookhouse, with a portion of oatmeal and rapidly solidifying fat in their bowls, he welcomed them to the dormitory with a stick in his hand: "Come here, you! Which is your bed?" And when they showed him, he banged the stick down on the top blanket. A cloud of dust flew up every time. The mining suits with the blue bands were kept on hooks behind the beds. Dust was a fault.

"Look at that filthy mess, and you call yourself human beings! Just look at that!" A further blow, and another cloud of dust proved that Death's-head was right. "Give me your name and number!" He gradually moved from one set of bunks to the next, and the same stereotyped conversation and the same banging with his cane was repeated. The prisoners stood at attention. The fat on the cooling oatmeal was turning into a waxy mealy substance. Outside, another unknown shift was marching over the concrete. Death's-head summoned the brigade leader, the storekeeper, and the guard in charge of the dormitories. The prisoners received a portion of their earnings from the pit. Approximately 13 per cent. The remainder was kept by the camp to cover the expenses of guarding, food, clothing, and heating. One of the punishments was the possibility of denying the prisoners their chance to buy things. The canteen was outside the wire, beside the guards' common room beyond the fence strip, and they went there to buy things once or twice a month. Soap, tobacco and cigarette papers, toothpaste, food. Stamps and writing paper.

Death's-head knew that the prisoners hated him, but he obviously reveled in a hatred accompanied by powerlessness. This was the same relationship that he had with his beautiful and sinful wife. It was rumored that, at home, he had to wash the dishes and scrub the floors. Any man would certainly have done this for a wife like his, but Death's-head suffered under it. When he was seeing to the cleanliness in the camp, the toilets, washrooms, stairs, and corridors were washed at least four times over. You could count on this, just as you could count on a sinking feeling in your stomach as the cage rushed down the shaft; when Death's-head learned this, it filled him with pride and satisfaction. He felt he was the king of all the animals.

The storekeeper was a fat sixty-year-old, one of the few fat men in the camp. The leader of a brass band with which he had given a few concerts without paying taxes. A few secret concerts with the aim of achieving a faster growth in his standard of living. Occasionally, he would make a joke about himself because of his fatness, saying that he was a display prisoner whom the camp leadership showed to delegations from abroad.

The brigade leader was forty and was serving his seventh sentence for car theft. He was so much of a professional jailbird that it was a little too much even for Death's-head. Anyhow, the Knight's gang went off duty in less than half an hour, and so he contented himself with a list of occupants of dusty beds and imperfectly cleaned boots. He issued a few gratuitous rebukes and uttered a couple of threats for the future.

The brigade leader listened to all this with a face just as serious as the situation demanded and then, by way of excuse, repeated several familiar sentences: "There are no cloakrooms, and it's not a good thing to keep mining clothes full of dust at your bedside. It's very difficult to wash the corridor down when we have no running water. The men and I try to cope with this, because we know that it angers you, sir." Et cetera, et cetera.

Then he called them to attention for Death's-head's departure.

Bobo, who throughout the inspection had been standing at the grille with the keys in his hand, let Death's-head pass, glared at the prisoner orderly, who had also called them to attention, as a sign of human solidarity or something similar, slammed the grille, locked up, and went away.

With this, an undisturbed evening could begin for the occupants of the hut. Or by now, rather, an undisturbed night. Only somewhere it had been decided that this was still not the end of today's events. In any case, after such an eventful day, there could not be a normal night. And the harassed Knight wanted to drink the blood from their hearts.

happenings

". . . He was one of those who leave their lairs by night
and raise their fists to sleeping windows,
dressed in scarlet velvet and gray steel."

Vojda was in the bunker by himself. They had come for him in the middle of the night, and before he could realize that he should or perhaps at least could have done a thousand different things, he was already walking through the space between the guards and was here. But each of the possibilities that later came into his head was no more than an idea from detective stories he had read. He was aware of this. There was nothing to be done, nothing at all. In this triple square of barbed wire that made a human being into a mere hut-dweller. Nothing at all. It was infuriating and hopeless, but unfortunately true.

It had begun with a hand touching the edge of his bed and with the vague awareness that a flashlight beam was shining on his face. He had realized that this feeling was not a dream. He had opened his eyes and had seen a row of high boots beside his bed in the light of the flashlight. The boots belonged to guards—he immediately remembered that they could not belong to anyone else. The omnipresent superior high boots. He was still trying to understand what he had to do with them just now. As a small boy, he used to go to the forest with his friends to collect bilberries, strawberries, and raspberries.

"My childhood has left me and gone away, there to the blue rocks . . ."

This song of Satchmo's had always reminded him in later life of the places of his childhood, and the homemade disc based on a recording from Radio Luxembourg was the showpiece of the record library of this unmarried lieutenant, who entertained the female warrant officers from air-traffic control in his room, because civilian ladies unfortunately could not get through the locked gate.

He came from an industrial village near Pilsen, and the forest had been part of an estate that had been taken over during the Occupation by Heydrich's widow. He had once been caught in the forest, together with several childhood friends, by a detachment of Hitler Youth. Daggers, black shorts, belts, banners and flags. And the forest of Heydrich's widow. Vojda had been barely seven years old at the time—he could no longer remember exactly—but he remembered how the Hitler Youth boys had beaten them, tied them up, and held them prisoner long into the night, and had it not been for a Czech forester who happened to pass that way, they might well have ended up tied on top of an anthill. They had been stealing the bilberries of Heydrich's widow. That moment had remained engraved in the lieutenant's mind with hatred and fear, feelings that breed and complement one another. He had so strong a dread of powerlessness that, very much later, when his friends at the pilot-training school had set up burning candles around his bed and played the *March of the Fallen Revolutionaries* on a tape recorder, he had almost had an hysterical seizure. When he had eventually realized he was not dead and it was all only a joke, he was seized by such a terrible rage that he had thrown the tape recorder at one of the jokers. It was state property, but all it cost Vojda was a black mark for discipline, because they had all then joined together with him to pay for the repair. The only punishment he had received at the flying school. Fear of powerlessness was his only weakness, a secret one, which he often had to struggle with.

Now, too, when he noticed the hand on the edge of his bed and then also on his body and the flashlight beam on his face, his first feeling, as soon as he was awake enough to be able to understand the connections, was that of his heart standing still and a sudden shudder in his arm.

"What's that?" he asked sharply. *"What's up?"* He hoped that Pilot would wake up, that anyone would wake up and that he would not be alone, against this row of dully gleaming boots in the darkness around him. You can go through anything in the world, provided you have a firm base of concordant feeling. Love, friendship, religion . . . or a political creed. An idea.

"Come along to the gate," a voice whispered out of the darkness. "Quick about it! And no noise!"

He reacted with complete confusion, mistrust, and a feeling of fear. He was outnumbered. It came over him like a feverish shiver. Moreover, the fire in the room had long since gone out, and now they pulled the blanket off him. St. Bartholomew's night? Of course, all that talk about the violence of our police. The bourgeoisie have police, but we have the security . . . Socialist legality. Here and there, something was revealed, here and there, it was true, something was explained in a whisper. The Communist pilot, Lieutenant Vojda, had never bothered himself with this. It had never particularly interested him.

"But why?"

An ungracious hand took him by the shoulder. Roughly and as a matter of routine.

"Don't ask questions! Just move!"

The shiver was now a real chill. He had already made out that there were four men around his bed. There was probably another standing at the door. A strip of pale light came from the corridor. He could even make out the black spots of the stamps on his underwear. One of the four was holding his blankets in his hand. He saw the truncheons, too—they shone dully, like the boots.

"Why should I have to go to the gate?" Someone must wake up. Someone at least must *know* that they've taken me away. That I haven't disappeared of my own accord. He looked into the corner where Havránek and Jarda were sleeping. The dark outlines of the bunks with clothes hanging over them. The bright patches formed by the helmets hanging ready for the morning.

"Get your boots on!" Then, when his boots fell out of his hand as they gave them to him: "Get your boots on, or go barefoot!" The flashlight now shone on his feet. Bare feet bound above the ankles with the bands of linen underpants. A stamp on each leg. "You can get your foot-bindings later!"

He snatched the bindings from the pile and stuffed them into the sleeve of his jacket.

"Trousers!"

He groped about at the side of the bed, and the torch followed his hands in their wanderings.

"Why should I have to go to the gate? What's happened?"

"The lieutenant wants to talk to you!"

"Get a move on, or we'll give you a hand!"

"Do you hear? Don't you understand?"

I'm completely alone, he realized.

"God, what the hell's going on?" a voice said in the darkness.

"We've got to go to work tomorrow, and you're ruining our sleep!"

This was a call to action, and a murmur of assent sounded from all sides of the dormitory.

"Which damned fool is waking us up?"

The light went out in a flash, and Vojda was seized under the arms by several pairs of hands.

"Let's go!"

"I'm barefoot," he shrieked. He only had had time to get one boot on. He attempted to grab the bed, but it was too late! It would have been useless anyway.

"You can sort that out at the gate!"

The door to the corridor formed a pale violet oblong of light from the bulbs on the ceiling. It dazzled him a little, and the stone floor of the passage was cold, as always. It was not until they were outside, after they had dragged him past the night orderly standing at attention by the table, and the entrance grille had been locked, that Drumstick gave him the boot and allowed him to put it on.

The Knight was waiting for them by the gate, right behind the death strip at the fence. He stood with his back to the lights in the fence strip. He was huge, powerful, and terrifying.

"So there you are, are you?" he said. He added a little scorn to his voice. "The hero! You won't tell many tales about that, eh?" He tweaked Vojda's upper lip with his index finger. Then he put his hands on his hips. There was a truncheon hanging from his right wrist. He spoke to the guards: "Put him in number nine!" He turned and walked away. By the time Vojda addressed him, he had his hand on the bars of the turnstile.

"Sir . . ."

The Knight turned his head and held out his hand to Drumstick: "Don't forget to give him the change of clothes!" He forced himself into the turnstile, and the bar banged up and fell again. For a moment, he was lit up by the lights in the death strip, and then he disappeared. The entrance to the guardhouse was at a slight angle.

Number nine meant the bunker, cell nine.

"Why should I have to go to the bunker?" asked Vojda.

"Come along!" Coathanger took him by the arm. "Don't do anything silly. You know it's not worth it!" Was there some element of sympathy and understanding in Coathanger? Or was he afraid, this subtle dried-out figure? A passing uniform.

"But I want to know why!" (God, it's a cold night.)

"Sort that one out with the lieutenant!"

Drumstick rushed up, turned Vojda by his shirt in the direction of the bunker door and prodded him in the ribs with his baton.

"No talking! Just move! *Do you understand?*" It was the same hysterical voice that had roared at Günther at the afternoon roll call. Vojda remembered Pilot saying: "Go on, Günther!"

He understood them. In fact, it was the only thing he understood perfectly. But he had no idea what going to the bunker involved. There had, of course, been the time in the pilot-training school when he had got a black mark for the smashed tape recorder, but his friends had protected him. I do it for you today—you do the same for me tomorrow. But even if Vojda had had any idea what going to the bunker involved, no amount of experience or well-tried practices would have helped him this time.

They stripped him naked, and then they returned his underclothes to him. If he had taken two shirts—a common trick when going to the bunker—they would have taken one from him. Then they issued him completely new trousers from the store—but they were only made of linen, not of the warmer hessian—a jacket, a vest, and a cap. Leggings. Everything was damp, with a faint smell of mold and dirt. It was a special store, only for the bunker, and, like the bunker, it was a little below ground level. But out of laziness most of the guards did not bother to use it. Responsibility for trousers, cap, et cetera. Making notes about them. And so it was possible to get into the bunker with two shirts. With a piece of blanket wrapped around your body. With some tobacco in your jacket lining. Cold also formed part of the punishment, and there was a thorough chill in the cells. There was never any heat. A concrete floor with a thin layer of eternally wet xylolite. The windows were not even glazed. Just a grille and a piece of metal a few inches thick with holes drilled in it. So small that no cigarettes or pieces of food could be passed through them. Hunger, too, was part of the punishment and the re-education of the new socialist man. Prisoners in the bunker were fed only once every three days. The days when Bobo was on bunker duty were an exception. Bobo served food every day, and, in return, the prisoners had to listen to the story of how he had missed his vocation, because he longed to be a military messenger. A devil sewn up in black leather and nailed to the saddle of a powerful motorcycle.

Number nine. The bunker section of the camp had just nine cells. All below ground level and a little damp. Number nine was positively wet. It lay at the lowest point. There was always water on the floor, and, with time, the xylolite had turned into red mud, clinging to their boots in lumps. Beside number one, a barred gate led to the corridor of the administration hut, a grille with a patent lock, and beyond number nine, there was a narrow toiletlike window onto the yard. The prisoners in number one could talk to people outside, when there happened to be no one patrolling. Several times, it had even proved possible to open the door of number one with a hooked pole. It was only locked on a bolt, like all the other cells. When this could be done, the prisoner from number one could distribute food and cigarettes to all the others.

Surprise and the feeling of goose flesh, which came upon him as though from biting cold, did not leave Vojda even after Drumstick and Coathanger had dragged him to number nine and locked the door behind him. He was surprised—even by the fact that it really was just as he had expected. The cell was empty, bare, with the marks of the hands and feet of many prisoners, who had scratched their way up to the window to look out through a hole in the bare and rusty metal. He had received a straw mattress and one blanket for the night. These, too, had come out of the bunker store, and they were damp. To crown it all, before he had managed to put it on the wooden bed, the mattress had slipped down behind the door and fallen into the red mud on the floor. When he picked it up and turned the soiled side downward on the bed, he noticed a peephole in the door. Drumstick or Coathanger was watching him.

A moment later, the reprimand came: "Go to sleep!" Then a switch clicked, and the light over his head went out. He was standing in the narrow space between the beds (there were two of them), immersed in total darkness. The holes in the window were not penetrable enough for the glow of the night sky and the camp lights to come in. He heard footsteps coming toward the door, then the peephole in the door banged, and more steps. For a moment, a band of light shone through the peephole. The grille to the corridor banged, and he could hear the sound of it being locked. And this time the band of light in the doorway disappeared, too, without any click from a switch too far away.

The cell. This had been what it was like in prison, awaiting trial, and awaiting the transport. He walked over to the wall and tapped a few letters in Morse.

No reply.

He tried again, with the same results.

Then he stood with his head against the door and shouted: "Havránek!" Pilot must, after all, be somewhere here, too. Of course, this was the Knight's punishment for the scene during roll call in the corridor. "Havránek!" He could not know what the Knight knew—that Pilot remembered more than just some blows at roll call. He remembered the first transport—after the Russian prisoners had vacated the camp in May 1945. He remembered other camps in whose yards there had been gallows, very similar to those on which the commandants of those camps had met their end, the commanding officers wearing the same uniform as the Knight. He remembered the dead, shot while attempting to escape. Even now, he had still not received any verdict, and all this was very strange. Vojda could not have known all this, because it had happened in the years when he was still at school. When he stood as a guard of honor at the bust of Stalin, when he was longing to get to the Žižka School, the pilot-training school, when he stood as a guard of honor at the bust of Stalin draped in black cloth. When he flew for the first time with his instructor, when he flew solo for the first time, when he first flew a jet, when the warrant officer from air-traffic control visited him for the first time in his room at the air-field and he was able to play her his Satchmo record. When he

went to a recording studio with his tape recording from Radio Luxembourg and got them to make the disc he had longed for—which
was not on sale, because only Russian songs, folk songs, and brass-
band music were on sale. And classical music, of course, classical
music. Only Vojda was not interested in that. He had tried for
some time, within the framework of his political training, to convince himself that he was interested in Russian songs and folk
music, because it was the art of the people and not a pseudo cul-
ture, but then he gave up and listened to Luxembourg like everyone
else. He had a feeling of enjoying forbidden fruit if he listened to it.
All this time, Pilot had spent behind wire; all this time, he had
been learning to react and be troublesome. All this time, he had
been preparing himself to be able to say to the parole board one
day: "Gentlemen, you can all kiss my ass! One, two, and three."

For this reason and for many others, Pilot was not in the
bunker. And from one of the neighboring cells came the unknown
voice of an unknown man. He was calling for peace and quiet. The
nocturnal voice of a man disturbed in his sleep.

Fear came over Vojda once again. Something he had fought
against since his early youth. Fear that he had been battling with
even when he had forced himself to raise his hand at the Knight's
question about further witnesses for Tomschin. And he should and
must in fact have been prepared for this when he had raised it. "I,
too, can testify at any time and any place. . . ." Any time. Here.
Any place. Here. But he lacked the experience, even though he had
seen so many films and read so many adventure stories about men
in situations similar to his present one, and even though he knew
that he would only get a slice of bread and a cup of substitute
coffee in the morning. All this only fulfilled old desires. But he
could not have been and was not prepared for the water on the
floor. For the deathly and demoralizing cold. His boots, with the
slushy xylolite stuck on them, were wet. He had forgotten the bindings in the sleeve of his other jacket and had not been issued an-

other set. When he took his boots off and lay down, he felt the wet cuffs of his trousers on his ankles. But without bindings his feet had been freezing in the boots. He rolled the lower edge of his trousers up, and rubbed his soles and toes together. He wrapped himself in the blanket as tightly as he could, but what they called a blanket was nothing but an old, worn-out, threadbare, and miserably narrow piece of cloth. He was determined to go to sleep and await what the future would bring with as much calmness as possible. He had to sleep. He knew that he would not even have this single miserable blanket in the daytime. He pulled his jacket collar up over his head and breathed under it. He rubbed his feet and arms again. But he still could not get his whole body warm at the same time. In the end, his weariness put him to sleep. His weariness from an eventful day, from the mine, and from the feeling of being hopelessly lost. If the Knight had been a psychologist, he could now have bought Vojda, just in return for taking him to a warm room full of people. But the Knight was only the Knight. And, as such, he could not know much about people, and nothing at all about people like Vojda.

When the camp public-address system announced reveille for the morning shifts, Havránek had long been sitting on his bed, dressed and smoking. A moment later, an orderly bawled reveille into the dormitory and put the lights on. On the top bunk, Jarda, too, was fully dressed, lying on folded blankets; he had his hands behind his head and was looking at the ceiling. They heard the orderly rushing along the passage from door to door. A moment before reveille, the guards had unlocked the grille in front of the hut entrance, as the orderlies had to go to the cookhouse for breakfast. A bowl of coffee—what passed for coffee here—and bread. A round loaf to every four men. The Knight's shift had already gone off duty, and the new shift did not have the Knight's reasons for being afraid of an uncontrollable camp. Apart from this, the camp was empty in the early morning, and there was not even a guard at the bunker yet.

Pilot finished his cigarette, stood up, and tugged Jarda's foot. "Let's go!"

Jarda kept a lookout. At first, until yesterday afternoon, he had been ready to believe that Vojda was a *provocateur*, an informant, or, at least, just *one of them*—one of those who have uniforms, weapons, and the power always to be right and always to have the last word. All that enthusiastic talk about Communists had got on his nerves even more than Vojda's behavior over the parcel. They reminded him too much of a school where the teachers never changed, but the curricula, the truths, and the lies changed overnight. What he considered to be truths and lies. This talk rang with the hypocrisy of all such declarations by professional tooth-extractors. Provided, of course, that their talk was made in a situation in which they needed to make a declaration. The Inquisition, too, had been inspired by faith. It had, of course, had a splendid excuse. While destroying the body, it was safeguarding the immortal soul. The murders carried out by the modern inquisitors lacked this reason. There was, of course, the matter for the whole people and similar holy obligations. And they applied just as much to the green uniforms of the guards as to Vojda's pilot's uniform. But all this was now far away, even though it was ever-present in the background here. Now there was only the fact that Pilot needed someone to keep watch for him at the bunker. For Pilot, Jarda would have kept watch even if the camp commandant himself had been sitting in the bunker, the once hard-working tailor from Brno and the now equally hard-working and conscientious commandant of the Corrective Labor Camp, who, for Jarda, as for most of the prisoners, represented a personification of the world of the long-toothed Bolshevik, the swine, the scoundrel, a man who had to be withstood simply in the interests of Jarda's humanity. If Jarda had been twenty years older, he would perhaps have been a member of the Communist Party, or at least a revolutionary. But then the hard-working little tailor would also have been a hard-working little tailor, and not the commandant of a camp and a bearer of ideas. Great, holy, and well-paid ideas. For every ton of coal extracted by the prisoners, the commandant also got a bonus.

And so Jarda stood, a moment later, leaning against the corner of the bunker, in the yard, nonchalantly rolling himself a cigarette and carefully watching the entrance to the camp, behind which was the guardhouse and behind which danger lurked.

Pilot walked under the windows of the cells, softly calling Günther's and Vojda's names. The German answered him from number five. Vojda from number nine.

"I'm here," said Günther, and the conversation could begin.

"Have they done anything to you?"

"No, only a little treatment. The usual beating."

"Have you got anything broken, any teeth knocked out? Bruises, lumps?"

"I'm so cut up from the coal down the pit, I'd never be able to pin it on them."

"Have you got a punishment order?"

"Yes."

"What for?"

"Refusing to obey an order."

The words were a code behind which developed concepts were hidden. Pilot stood below with his head thrown back, and Günther scrambled up to the covered window. Even so, his voice sounded muffled, as though it came from another world.

"Are they threatening you with the prosecutor?"

"Yes."

"Demand an interview with him alone, when you go for report. The Knight's got to pass it on. You've got witnesses."

"I've already been for report."

"Then demand pen and paper and put your request in writing."

"O.K."

"Do it that way."

"I will."

"Write it as a complaint about unjustified force and lowering of human dignity. And if you feel up to it, go on a hunger strike."

"O.K."

"We'll send you some food in the rags." Food in the rags was one of the few ways of smuggling it into the bunker. The parcel was concealed inside a floor cloth and thrown through the window onto a pile of cloths and worn brushes at the end of the corridor. Every morning, the prisoners in the bunker cleaned up. The guard opened the cells, and the prisoners took the brushes and cloths from the pile.

"Anything else you want?"

"No," replied Günther's muffled voice, which was followed by a thud as he leaped down from the narrow ledge behind the boarded window onto the floor of the cell.

"Good-bye!"

"Good-bye, Pilot. Thanks."

You could picture Günther lying down and wrapping himself up in his blanket again. Sleep and warmth were enclaves of freedom inside every prisoner. Reveille for the morning shifts was an hour and a quarter before general reveille. And even if it had only been five minutes, the idea that it was not worth lying down any more did not apply here, the idea you used at home sometimes when you had extended the night to the early morning. "What I sleep through, I don't serve."

Vojda heard Pilot's voice in his frozen half-sleep. He recognized it instantly, leaped up regardless of the cold, and tried to get to the window. But the wall was worn too smooth from the attempts of his predecessors, and Vojda was too small to be able to reach up to the edge of the ledge in order to pull himself up. He repeated his desperate attempts again and again. He even put the mattress upright under the window and tried to use it as a ladder. But it was a vain attempt. And both the beds were fixed, built of brick with a firmly attached layer of boards on top. He had heard Pilot's conversation with Günther, but unintelligibly.

"Try and climb up," Pilot called to him under his window. "Ludvík! Climb up to the window!"

"I can't," he shouted desperately. "I can't make it!" He heard Pilot cursing. A moment later, he heard someone scratching at his window from outside. Pilot was hanging by his fingers from the edge of the roof, and Jarda, who had helped him up, had returned to his post at the corner.

"Ludvík, I'm here."

"Yes," called Vojda. He was standing astride the beds.

"How are you?"

"Pretty well, but the cold is awful."

"You'll have to get used to it."

"They've taken my clothes."

"Tear off a piece of blanket in the morning and wrap it around you."

"I'll try." He knew that he could not do it. Several people had already put the blanket to this use, and if he did it, there would be nothing left of it but a scarf.

"Have you had a punishment order?"

"A what?" The code was no use in Vojda's case.

"*You must have a punishment order!*" Pilot scraped his feet along the wall. "You can't be in the bunker without a punishment order, that's a regulation." A formality that was not observed. But it existed to be observed, devised for the benefit of the guards as much as the prisoners, and Pilot was not a man capable of forgiving and forgetting. He had nothing to be afraid of and could afford it. And you could fight against a written formulation of the reasons for the punishment. The reasons could be refuted. "Do you understand? You must have a punishment order. You must know the reason why they've thrown you into the bunker."

"Very well."

"Demand an interview with the prosecutor." His feet groped again along the wall outside. Pilot weighed more than a hundred and seventy pounds, a hundred and seventy pounds hanging by the first joints of his fingers gripped around the zinc gutter. "Could you manage a hunger strike?"

He had to repeat each sentence several times before Vojda grasped the sense of it.

"I've never tried it before." Hunger strike. It had never entered Ludvík's head, not even in a dream, that he might perhaps one day be part of a world that had hunger strikes. But the world is all the same place, and man cannot get out of it alive.

"*Try!*" The hunger strike is the last isolated weapon of the prisoner. One prisoner, of course, did not matter. Nor did ten or even a hundred prisoners. There had been thousands whose heads had been smashed to pieces, yet who, according to the official record, had died of a lung inflammation. There had been men who had had their genitals torn up during interrogation and bones dislocated, and yet had been shot while attempting to escape. There had been men who disappeared. Completely and without trace. But the hunger strike was the will of the prisoner. The ultimate exertion, a self-denial, a punishment worthy of Goethe's young Werther, and not being in control and breaking the prisoner's will got the guards a bad report. There was also a difference between the interrogators, who crippled, killed, prepared material for the gallows and citizens for jail at the will and whim of the powerful and the all-powerful, and the guards, the least of the great, who merely guarded the prisoners.

"You'll always have some food in the cloths under the window."

"Where?"

"Outside in the corridor. You'll see it when you hand in your mattress. . . ."

The roof sloped slightly to the yard, and the gutter was slipping from under Pilot's fingers. This always meant hanging for a moment by one hand, by the four fingers of one hand, and then changing hands.

"Don't forget about the punishment order! Or the interview with the prosecutor! Request it first thing in the morning! And don't be afraid! Do you understand? Don't be afraid!"

"Yes." It was easier not to be afraid now. There were friends here, friends who did fantastic things just to quell this feeling of fear in him. Vojda sensed he would not be afraid. This was his life. His own.

Pilot realized with relief that he need say no more. He could do everything else all by himself. He let go and dropped onto the wet gravel four yards below. He felt his fingers coming back to life. He knew, of course, that their conversation had been listened to and more or less heard by the occupants of all the surrounding cells. But he had to risk it. Even that someone might have been listening who should not have been. There was no other way, and there were very rarely informants sitting in the bunker. People were sent there according to the choice of the guards. They were not nice characters, usually. The camp had long ago lost the political character it had had at the time when Pilot Havránek arrived there in the first transport. Today, most of its inmates would have been in prison, whatever the regime in the country. No, they were not nice characters, they really could not be described as such—but in reliability, they were among the best. Hard, because the world had been hard on them and they had had no choice but to harden even more or perish. Either in a strait jacket in sick bay or of their own accord. But sick bay did not take people in every day, and somewhere inside them and outside them and outside the wire that separated them from the world there still existed the principles, the hopes, and the people who allowed them to be hard.

Pilot picked himself up from the gravel. He heard Vojda's muffled voice again, saying good-bye. He could picture him. Lieutenant Ludvík Vojda. Prisoner Ludvík Vojda. His man, yes, he knew for certain, today he knew it, his man belonged to another generation and was on the other side, but nonetheless he was a man, even though he had sat in a different plane and behind a different control column. Perhaps his was another truth than that for which Havránek used to shoot down German planes and V–1s, but nonetheless he was *his* man, and they both belonged to this country. They were the same.

He came up to Jarda at the corner. "All over. Let's go for breakfast."

Ahead of them lay the lifeless, illuminated gatehouse; in the distance they could hear a faint snarl of engines and knew that it was the trucks coming to take them to work. As soon as the trucks arrived, the loud-speaker at the gate would order first readiness and then, five minutes later, parade for work. They started running to the hut.

Someone anonymous had already brought them a bowl of substitute coffee with rings of grease floating on it from a badly washed pan. It was hot and bitter, and before they had finished drinking it, the loud-speakers ordered them to prepare for work. They took their laminated helmets and working gloves from the hooks behind their beds. A moment later, they were sauntering out in a drawn-out line. Over the camp lay a pale and unpleasant gloom, broken now by the fading lights in the death strip and the rest of the camp. The gray morning at the moment that turns all the women in the world into nothing more than unpleasant creatures. Light clouds scudded across the sky.

The brigade leader formed them up in fives, according to their numbers. Havránek stood at the front. They lined up in silence. Everyone knew his place by now.

Then the loud-speaker ordered parade and they marched out to the gate.

The Knight had been relieved on guard duty by Brawny. His second nickname was just as funny—Porker—and he had come by both of them because of his fatness. He was one of those fat men who rarely lose their composure, who like a quiet life, comfort, and good food. And, of course, beer. Beer, in fact, first and foremost. And people who gave him peace.

When the morning shifts had gone off to the mine and the guard now on duty at the bunker came to report that a man called Vojda was demanding a punishment order and an interview with the prosecutor, he flipped through a folder marked "Bunker," where the food coupons and punishment orders of prisoners in the bunker were kept, and finding nothing with Vojda's name on it, he asked for the man's number. The number formed the personality of a prisoner much more than his name. There were different prisoners with the same name. The number always provided a distinction. The bunker guard had providently written down Vojda's number.

Brawny reflected for a moment. The number was three days old. Then he looked through the folder again. On the occasions, the very rare occasions, when he broke with his character as a well-meaning fat man, he could be rough, too, and he and the Knight had never liked one another. A prisoner without a punishment order had no business being in the bunker. Especially a prisoner who had been put there by the Knight. He held the folder in his hand for a moment, then threw it on the table and said: "Let the man out! There's nothing here. Another mess!"

The guard went off with the keys in his hand, pushed his way through the turnstile and disappeared into the corridor of the administration hut. Two minutes later, Vojda was again in his dormitory. The shift had gone, and he knew that he could sleep now till nine. After nine, a morning count was ordered, a roll call for the afternoon and night shifts. He did not believe that the whole affair of Günther, Pilot, and his raising his hand at the Knight's question was over by any means. He would have been glad if it were over, but he realized that it was not over for the Knight, and thus it was not over for him either. It could not be over if it was not over for the Knight and by the Knight's hand. This was not the confrontation in which Buffalo Bill and the badmen both stood with their hands on their holsters. It was a definite confrontation, like the one that ran through all society, but apart from the immediate participants, it was still not clear who was the badman and who was Buffalo Bill. Or at least the lawman, represented by the sheriff's star and the will of all the others—naturally, by the will of all the others.

He had to reflect who the Knight was and what he represented. He knew that for him personally he now represented an enemy, a danger. But otherwise? The guards? The society that paid them? The philosophy of this society? He suddenly felt how foreign all these things were to him, now that he was no longer lying on his bed in his room at the airfield or sitting at a preflight briefing with his flying suit unzipped. He longed to sleep with pretty girls and longed to get rid of his existential worries. In both, he had so far only been partially successful. But even though there was more that he did not know and could only sense and guess, he knew for certain that this was not only a confrontation between him and the Knight, that it was at the same time a confrontation—a confrontation into which he had entered voluntarily—between what the Knight and all like him thought of life and what Vojda, Pilot, Jarda, and certainly a whole mass of other people thought of it. He included here his former comrades from the airfield, his professional colleagues, and necessarily also his true friends and the war-

rant officers from air-traffic control who occasionally visited him
and to whom he played Satchmo. What religion we belong to does
not matter. People are either good or bad. Perfect or helpless, helpless in one of those feelings between goodness and its opposite.

Meanwhile, he was satisfied at getting his hessian clothes back
from the store, at being able to heat his body, after the linen
bunker clothes, in warm water, which, by some mysterious chance,
was still running, to dry his boots and his feet, to crawl between the
blankets and warm his frozen body, to lie down, to sleep. He could
not say that he had ever needed all this more than now, and he
could not have said that he needed anything else at all. The world
can, in fact, be quite good in a sense. If any memory had remained
in him, any remnant of his nocturnal depression, then it was only
his shame. And he was glad that no one knew about his feelings.

At noon, the Knight came on duty again. Perhaps it was written and preordained somewhere that Vojda should be the unfortu-
nate object of the row that could now fully explode between the
Knight and Porker. That was how it happened. Porker, in the end,
threw the notebook with the bunker strength down in the middle of
the table and said very angrily: "What's all this, you damned fool,
putting people away without papers? There are some regulations in
force here, you know. If a man's done something, I write it down,
and that's that. But I don't make a big mess of it!" He glared at
the Knight through the lenses of his glasses. He slapped the report
book with the back of his hand, and his voice grew louder: "You
fool, you've really made me see red! The sloppiness of it! How will
I ever get on with anyone here!" He had always been a conscientious official. And now he was angry, and he was glad that it was
the Knight that he had an excuse to curse.

"I simply forgot to file it," the Knight stammered. (They're
getting at me again. I've put my foot in it again.) "I've got it."

This, of course, was not true. Anyway, the punishment order

was not a matter of any weight, though, of course, they should be entered—there was a regulation to that effect. By chance, it had not been entered. And, by the same chance, Porker had taken exception to this. The same chance by which he later remembered Vojda's air-force uniform, the same chance that had guided his feelings toward the Knight, as the feelings of a small, fat man toward a tall man. Vojda was still slightly smaller than Brawny, and there had never been any quarrel between him and Brawny, nor could there have been—he had not been in the camp long enough. If he had any quarrel with the Knight . . .

"What the hell do I care whether you have it, for Christ's sake!" He again struck the report book with the back of his hand. "What the devil do I care that you have it! It should be in here!" He struck it again. *"HERE!"* He went red and then blue in the face. "Well, it's your own mess. Nothing else. A big mess!"

Getting into a big mess was not conducive to the honor of a guard. Although Porker held the shortest roll-call parades of all the camp's shift commanders, the shortest parades that could possibly exist—whether out of kindness, reason, or laziness was not known —he had never got into a mess. His count always tallied, and if he missed one or two people, he had faith in the fence strip and the death belt and did not get excited about it. In general, he wished people peace and quiet, and fate perhaps gave him peace and quiet in return.

Five minutes after the change-over—Brawny had still not packed his shoulder strap and pistol into his briefcase—the camp loud-speakers were already calling Vojda's name. He was called three times, and only when he did not come to the gate even then did Coathanger and Bobo set out into the camp to find the evader. The Knight never forgot. He also knew about Havránek's low number. The number that aroused respect and shame, if these feelings had any place in the Knight. The experience acquired in years and years of camp life. The incident with the parole board. Perhaps also fear of the hardness that must lie behind the number of the man they called Pilot. He had spent so long here and evidently lived above him and above them. In his case, the Knight had to await his opportunity. Some disorder in his personal affairs, bad work output, indiscipline, jumping the food line. The parole board incident was so famous (apart from the matter of Havránek's verdict itself) that it caused even the commandant to treat him with reserve. And the Knight always respected the reserve of all his commandants.

high
noon

Two shots rang out almost simultaneously.
Pete lay strangely hunched up, and blood seeped out under
his white glove. He again tried to close his hand on the pistol,
and his legs jerked several times.

—*Fragment of an otherwise forgotten Western.*

Vojda did not hear the loud-speaker. He was asleep. By some chance—not an unusual occurrence in the case of Porker —no one had missed him at the morning roll call, and the loud-speaker announcement did not wake him up. He remained forgotten.

When now, for the second time in twelve hours, the blanket was pulled off him and Coathanger took him by the arm, he knew immediately what it was all about. It was just as unpleasant as it had been in the night, even though outside the midday sun was shining brightly, creating an atmosphere far from that of any Inquisition or secret court. He thought of the slushy floor of the bunker, of the icy cold that would again penetrate his body, of the gloom, with the dots of light in the metal in the window. He needed a moment to get control of himself. This time, Coathanger was alone. Bobo had avoided him somewhere on the way, and Coathanger never gave the impression of being an excessively frightening character. He had the appearance of a signalman at some provincial station whose retirement was long overdue.

"Well, up you get," he said. "Get up! Don't you hear?" His slightly weepy voice aroused a feeling of burdensome pity.

The door opened, and Death's-head came in: "Is he here?"

"Yes," Coathanger replied. "He's sleeping. Well, come on, get up, Vojda!"

Death's-head came up to the bed, and Vojda stared at both of them. He had opened his eyes when they woke him, but he did not speak or move at all. He again pictured the store with its damp clothes, the corridor with the mattresses against the back wall, the bolts on the doors. . . . Hearing stories about it and experiencing it for yourself were two different things. *Being in it yourself.* The powerlessness of the feeling of being in it. Then he realized that he was not alone. He was powerless, of course. Restricted by Coathanger, Death's-head, the Knight, the camp; within these limits and the legal setup that went hand in hand with them, their power and will prevailed. But their right was not infinite, it was not without qualifications, and it did not cease the moment the door of the bunker closed behind him. So it was not yet over. The Knight had not finished. There was no "We'll forget about it." The Knight had not forgotten, but, in doing so, he forced them not to forget it either (he now included Pilot, Jarda, and perhaps the whole dormitory, except for the apartment speculator, in the sphere of people who belonged to him). *He had not forgotten.* Yes, he forced them not to forget. He felt a mild satisfaction at being part of something moving forward, just as mysteriously and regularly as the earth. He watched the two men over him calmly and with a sudden serenity. Acquaintance with the cells was like acquaintance with the cat-o'-nine-tails. Once a man is broken in a certain way, he ceases to feel. The purpose of the bunker was to break people. He knew this already and realized that his first stay there had been a vaccination against smallpox. He had become immune.

"What's up?" he asked. "Why have you woken me up?" Of course, he hated the two men standing over him. They probably knew it and perhaps thought it was all right that way. As people, Coathanger and Death's-head meant nothing to Vojda. He hated them from the depths of his heart for standing here. On behalf of society, on behalf of the same society whose justice he believed in, a society which he had always pictured without hatred and which he had still been protecting only just over a month ago with his MIG-17.

"Reveille," said Coathanger gleefully. His intonation was that of the boys at school who deliberately told tales. Perhaps Coathanger had done so as well. It looked as though he had always been a stinker and perhaps took revenge on those who were not stinkers. Death's-head's presence had also suddenly taken away his weepiness and made him fiery. He began to spit out words like a machine gun. "Get up! Hup! Hup! Hup! Let's have you down! How many times have I got to tell you? Come on, quick!" He tapped Vojda with his baton. "Well!"

"Don't hit me!" said Vojda. "Why should I have to get up?"

"You can sort that out with the lieutenant. You're going to the bunker. Didn't get out of it after all, did you?" The authorities covered themselves, as always. The Knight behind Coathanger. The commandant behind the Knight. The higher commander behind the camp and the commandant. The ministry behind the higher commander. Society. The system. Offices, letters, orders. The law. And people, of course, people, too. Who was now in Vojda's place in his MIG-17?

"Take your soap and toothbrush with you," Death's-head advised him.

Vojda sat up. He would actually have preferred to sleep. He could not get rid of this feeling.

"I haven't got any," he said. "I only came the day before yesterday, and I haven't had anything yet to buy them with."

"Well, well, fancy that." Coathanger's voice was filled with the concern of a father for a child who is a failure. "You've been here three days, and you're going to the bunker already. Nice way you're starting off."

Vojda did not reply. He thought that Coathanger should keep this talk to himself. If he had to speak, he should at least stop talking nonsense and send him to the Knight. But the simplest thing was to keep quiet. Anyway, silence was assumed as an integral part of the re-education process. You can think what you like, but keep your thoughts to yourself. Don't force us to take it up with you.

"You'll want to go home on parole, won't you? But you don't know to behave!" He saw Vojda's face and fell silent, like a man whose well-meant advice, given from the depths of his pure heart, falls on unfertile ground. Vojda folded his sheets and blankets and could not help smiling as he did so. He had suddenly remembered how Daniel had addressed a guard as re-educator instead of sir. It seemed to him that there was something in this.

"Come on, don't hold us up," said Coathanger. "We haven't got all day to spend on you." He clicked his tongue in anger. "That's dreadful!"

Death's-head looked on icily and without involvement, as always. The absent gaze of Dracula or Frankenstein. He examined the dwarfs modeled from bread and toothpaste and exhibited on the shelf with the tin dishes.

What if I told him not to be so superior? Vojda suddenly thought. He took his towel from the wire hook on his bed and they went out. But they did not take him to the gate. They walked straight toward the bunker.

"Just a moment!" He turned to Coathanger. "What about my punishment order?"

"Sort that out with the lieutenant!"

"We'll have to go to the gate then." He was determined not to give in. Pilot had advised him. He wished he were like Pilot. Pilot was certainty. A model. An airman.

"You can phone from the bunker."

"I want to see the punishment order, sir." He felt himself gripped by nervousness, a tightening of his stomach at Coathanger's stupidity, his reluctance and fear as a subordinate little jailer to come before the eyes of his superior, the Knight. He overcame

the stomach nerves and forced himself to pitch his voice in a pleading tone: "Please take me there, sir."

Death's-head had detached himself from them and was marching across the yard toward the water tower. Coathanger looked
after him helplessly. He was all alone in this fix.

"Come on!" He waved his raised index finger without expression and made a weak attempt to take Vojda by the sleeve. "You
can't go to the gate."

"What about the key? I've got to hand the key in at the gate!"
It was true. Vojda had locked up.

Coathanger could not force him. He was too much of a weakling
to be able to. They went. The Knight spotted them approaching
immediately and went out to meet them in front of the fence strip.
At exactly the spot where they had met the evening before.

Vojda was not tall, and the Knight had to lower his head a
great deal in order to be able to peer searchingly into his face. On
his pink face he had some whiskers missed by his razor and a small
red cut on his cheekbone. He was rubbing it with his fingers.

"Well, what's the matter?" he demanded. He narrowed his eyes
like a cat in the sunlight and ran his fingers around the cut. "What,
what, come to have a little chat, have you?"

"Sir, I request you to inform me of the reason for my confinement to the bunker."

"You'll find out." He had the punishment order already filled
in. One or ten such punishment orders. That was no problem. In
the guardhouse, they had a drawer full of them, you only had to
write the name in. To write names from dawn to dusk. If there had
been enough bunkers, of course. Vojda's punishment order now
stated that he had behaved improperly in that he had shrieked
threats at a member of the guard shift. It was signed by the Knight
per and pro the camp commandant. He was authorized to do this
and he knew that, in the interests of discipline, the commandant
would not countermand his decision once Vojda was in the cell and

the whole bureaucratic machinery of the camp administration had got him into its clutches. In the bunker, a prisoner was charged twenty-five crowns a day for food and accommodation. And a two hundred crown fine for each work shift missed. But he did not want to tell Vojda the stated reason for the punishment now, simply because this little air-force lieutenant who had run a man over with alcohol in his blood might possibly prepare some arguments. He did not want to tell him because he knew the reason was false. The Knight knew he was lying. (He certainly stole, too.)

"I would like to speak to the commandant!" said Vojda. He had no illusions about the commandant. He was certainly not a just Lord God Almighty who rewarded good and punished evil. But he wanted the commandant involved. In such a way that he would have to admit one day; *I knew about it,* when he was questioned about the case. *Who* or *when*—this was beyond the scope of Vojda's immediate idea. But it was not important either. After the commandant would come the prosecutor. In his political training, he had often heard the sentence: "Comrades, you must ask questions, and you must ask them at the top of your voice." He was convinced that everything in the world was a problem of questions and answers. Until recently, the lessons from the political meetings had been to him something like the indispensable sense of life, though he had made an exception for his Satchmo record. The sense that we recognize even if we cannot understand it. Apart from this, an interview with the commandant was, as he had read that morning in the camp regulations hung up in the hut, something that he had a *right* to demand. Only when this institution had failed could he proceed further. It was his right, not a right that he had invented himself or one that might perhaps have been invented with his consent by others. He had not voted for it. He had not confirmed it. But there it was. It had descended from heaven together with all the Knights, Coathangers, Death's-heads and commandants, who, though they were part of it, yet never recognized or acknowledged it. The trick lay in forcing them to put him down just as they demanded. Vojda did not think of his right as a demand on society or as an attack on society. It was merely an attempt to get things done properly, and an innate sense of fair play.

The Knight looked at him in silence for a moment. It seemed that he was about to explode, but he gained control of himself. The word "right" did not do him good.

"I'm not your servant," he said in an unusually soft voice. "The commandant is over there, see? Go and see him over there!" He pointed a finger stretched out in front of his stomach at the first yard. The commandant, a small, fat, bald man, really was there. But between them was the wire and the belt of white sand. And right by the Knight's arm a board with the inscription: STOP! SHOOTING BELT! SHOOTING WITHOUT WARNING!

There were similar boards every fifteen yards along the whole inner side of the strip, and Ludvík—in the course of the three weeks he had spent in prison and his three days in the camp—knew and had heard enough to know how it would end if he ever had an urge to cross, even only with one foot, the boundary of the strip strewn with white sand.

The Knight plucked at his face nervously and left the cut alone: "Well!"

"Sir, I wish to know why I am being punished by confinement to the bunker!"

"You know only too well!"

"Could you please spell it out for me?"

"What?"

"Don't irritate the lieutenant!" Coathanger rebuked him.

For a moment, they were all silent again.

"I should like to see the punishment order, to know the reasons . . ."

"You are not going to know anything! Do you understand? *Do you understand?*" The Knight was at boiling point. This rebelliousness. A right indeed. The words "I want," "I demand," "I have the right"—these always made him boil.

"I demand an interview with the commandant and the prosecutor!"

The Knight roared. The prisoners were a malevolent lot, a crafty gang of depraved scoundrels who had decided to make things difficult for him. They drank his heart's blood and, in a mysterious way, were undermining his position, ruining the mission to which he had sacrificed everything. He seemed like a lover reproaching the world for not sharing his rapture. From the windows of the administration hut, the prisoners from the accounting department were looking in this direction. Coathanger stood beside the Knight. There was also someone standing behind Vojda's back, obviously waiting for the Knight to finish with him. Ludvík could not see the man behind him; he just sensed there was someone there.

"Dismiss to the bunker!"

"I demand the punishment order."

"Obey your orders!" The Knight drew himself up. "Are you refusing to carry out an order?"

"Don't irritate the lieutenant!" Coathanger. The damn idiot.

"I have a right to know . . ."

"Obey your orders!" There was no lawlessness. There were no rules, except the one that said you must obey orders. Not obeying an order was insubordination. Insubordination was punishable.

"Come on," said the stupid Coathanger mildly and timidly, as he pulled Vojda by the jacket. The Knight stood over them, enraged and inflated.

O.K. All right, thought Vojda. He looked straight into the Knight's face. You rotten cow. I hope you know I think you're a rotten holy cow. I won't sort it all out with you now, but I'll drink your blood yet. . . . He did not feel certain without Pilot, but as

long as he was doing no more than Pilot wanted, it seemed that it
had its importance.

"Come on! Do you understand?"

"Go on, man. Go on."

He turned and walked away. He was calm. The second round
was his, even though he was going to the bunker. He stepped aside
to avoid the man behind him. He saw it was a prisoner with his cap
in his hand and heard the Knight shriek at him: "What do you
want? I'll teach you to grin at me!"

A garbled reply from the prisoner, a "Please, sir," and then the
Knight roared again at the top of his voice: "Name?"

"Prisoner Hampl, sir."

"I'll teach you to grin in front of me! Orderly!" And when
Drumstick rushed from the gate after further calls: "Three days
bunker."

Hampl had been a juvenile delinquent who had recently turned
eighteen, and he had then been transferred from a juvenile re-
education center to an adult re-education center.

Coathanger, after the necessary clothes-changing and searching
procedure, slammed the door of number nine behind them and
bolted it. He had not yet left the corridor, they had not yet heard
the clanking and locking of the grille, before Vojda was standing at
the bell and pressing it.

"Hell," said Hampl, scowling. "Three days, because he said I
was grinning." He was not protesting. He was just amazed. He had
got used to not protesting during two years of corrective detention.
"Three days." He shook his head and spat into the toilet in the
corner. He was one of those people who reconcile themselves to
injustices by the belief that they always have all they possibly can
on their side. A path leads this way to modesty.

"I heard," answered Vojda. He was still pressing the bell vigor-
ously.

"Perhaps it doesn't ring. They never rang in Past'ák." Past'ák was the name given to the center for disturbed juveniles, which Hampl knew thoroughly.

Vojda shrugged his shoulders: "I'll keep it up for a while longer." Then, with his nail, he scraped a piece of insulation from the wires above the button and connected them. "It's O.K.," he shouted enthusiastically. "It's O.K. There's juice there." And then he joined them properly. He sat down on one of the beds. "And I don't need to keep pressing now." There was a roguish joy in him at this revenge for his interrupted sleep.

"Hey, you'll have them coming here!" Hampl did not understand. He always tried to be as far away as possible from the supervision of the guards.

"That's just what I want."

After a few minutes, the door to the corridor clattered, and then the bolt on their door was drawn. Coathanger came in and looked at Vojda with a hurt expression. He separated the wires uneasily. He waved his baton. "If they made you pay for it, then you'd look silly, wouldn't you?" He pointed to the wires.

"It was already like that, sir," Hampl was quick to reply.

"I know, it was already like that. You were, too, weren't you?" Then he turned to Vojda (the youth and Vojda were standing at attention, each on one of the beds): "The Lieutenant orders you to stop this!"

"I only want my punishment order, sir, and I cannot live with this water here."

"This isn't a cell, it's a mud bath," Hampl added.

Coathanger looked at the floor. He had perhaps originally wanted to take a step nearer, and then, seeing the morass beyond the threshold, he had second thoughts: "I tell you something. You're very obstinate, do you know? Get rid of it while there's still time. You're still young, and you won't get very far with that, I tell you. You'll get nowhere with that kind of obstinacy."

"Very well, sir." Vojda nodded. "But, all the same, I'd like that punishment order. I have a right to see it." He looked into Coathanger's face and saw nothing more than a wretched, downtrodden, and worn-out muzhik, a little weakling of a man ruined perhaps by all the kinds of misfortune that can come a man's way. But this little man had duties, and one of them was Vojda. The suppressed Ludvík Vojda.

"I'm giving you good advice; another man would get tough with you." Coathanger's voice was again full of blame, and he looked at Vojda reproachfully. Vojda was making things difficult for him. He had to go before the Knight's eyes again. He had always had a tendency toward sentimentality, and now, too, he felt sorry. He had rushed from the gate to the bunker and back again while Death's-head was sunbathing on the water tower. "I'm warning you, the lieutenant has had just about enough of you. Just watch your step!" The lieutenant was an authority similar to the evil witch who forces young children to eat their soup. But even if the soup is not eaten up, the evil witch never comes.

Coathanger slammed the door and went away. The grille to the corridor clanked.

Vojda shrugged his shoulders and connected the two wires again. Somewhere below them, six or seven hundred yards underground, Pilot was sitting at his mine engine, Jarda, too, and a whole crowd of people who he knew were thinking of him. He had to prove himself. To himself as well.

"I'd quit that," said Hampl. Coathanger had put the lights out as he went away, and they had both changed into mere black silhouettes against the lighter wall.

"How long have you got?" asked Hampl.

"Seventeen meters to go."

"Have you had parole yet?"

"No. Have you?"

"No, in three lousy years' time."

They were silent for a moment. It struck Hampl that he had in fact been sent to the bunker on account of Ludvík, because Ludvík had whipped up the Knight's rage. He had only been trying to give a message to the lieutenant from the camp doctor. The lieutenant was to come for an injection. And Hampl had enough misfortunes of his own (that attempt always to have as much as possible on his side).

"How long have you got altogether?" he asked, touching his elbow.

"Eighteen!"

"Springs?"

"No, meters." Springs were years, and meters were months.

"That's all!" He waved his hand scornfully. "I've got five springs."

That's nothing. You'll get rid of that on the toilet. That's no sentence. Vojda had heard talk like this a hundred times since the moment the gate of the prison closed behind him and he met the first prisoner. He had even heard it from his lawyer, who had come to shake hands with him after sentence was passed. For all of them, he was like a peculiar, insignificant beast from the last page of some nature-study book. How many children would be born over eighteen months? How many times in this period do we eat, sleep, make love, go to the theater, watch television, lie stretched out along a swimming pool? How many beautiful women, who force us to behold them merely by virtue of what they are, would we meet? This period of time. A time long enough for a woman to give birth twice over. A child born somewhere that night when the light had first shone in his eyes, after all the time in prison and during which he had made himself comfortable on the floor on a broken bed frame, a child born that night would be walking and talking when he came out again. The girls from their sponsored Pioneer detachment, who came to the airfield on Airman's Day, would in the meantime have become perfect girls, girls capable of receiving love. Every day, every hour of life is irreplaceable—but he recognized that his miserable eighteen months was only an illusion worthy of a spit and a contemptuous wave of the hand, that in jail were heroes of the same type as this Hampl, who measured his manliness by the years spent in prison, that it was also nothing for Pilot, who had already spent many times eighteen months here. But to his surprise, he had heard no such remark from Pilot.

The gate from the corridor clanked again. Violently and threateningly. They heard the steps of many feet—it was not the timid Coathanger. The switch clicked, and the peephole in their door turned into an arc of light. Then the footsteps stopped right on the threshold. The light on the ceiling went on, too, the door flew open, and the Knight walked in. He had to stoop a little in the doorway. He straightened up once he was inside. He did not care about the red slush at his feet. The passage behind him was full of guards. And from his wrist a truncheon was dangling by the strap.

Vojda and Hampl stood at attention on the beds. There really was a little too much water on the floor, even though the Knight himself was standing in this morass.

"Get down!" said the Knight; then he turned around and wrenched out the bell wires. Some plaster fell, and the button remained hanging a little on one side.

They got down.

"Well, what about your report? Who's going to report?"

"Bunker number nine, sir. Strength two prisoners," Hampl said slowly.

The Knight addressed himself to Vojda: "Listen, you . . . did you not understand the message the guard gave you?"

Vojda raised a foot and pointed to the lump of wet red mud on it.

"I can't stay here," he said. "And I want to know the reason for this punishment!" He began to realize that it was no longer a matter of Tomschin at all.

"I warn you, Vojda. *Lay off that!*" the Knight said. From the passage, Coathanger, Drumstick, Death's-head, and another unknown person looked on.

"We can get tough with you as well," said this anonymous character in the passage.

Yes, that's the way to drink the blood right from their hearts, Vojda suddenly thought. The law is a double-ended stick, like every stick, and if you're down, play strictly fair and take care and force the others—come what may—to do so, even though they have the advantage of power.

"I demand to be allowed an interview with the commandant, and I demand that the prosecutor should be informed."

"You've got nothing to demand here!" The stomach behind the belt heaved violently up and down. "Where do you think you are, eh?"

Vojda had graduated from scores of debates in the forces. Where we are. Our order. Our society. Our great age. The world in which we live. But he had never said what he said now; he spoke slowly and calmly. Very slowly, articulating the syllables carefully.

"In the twentieth century. In Europe. In a socialist state. In a corrective labor camp. In the bunker." He saw the Rider losing his equilibrium. But he could not yield now and melt away from the whole business, as he had from the parcel of sausage. This time, though, he knew what was involved. And he was in it, he was too much in it to be able to melt away, for them to allow him to retreat. He had seen how they hit Tomschin. He knew it was forbidden to beat people in our country. "I cannot refuse to accept the punishment—but please put me in another cell. And please inform the prosecutor."

"You will stay *here!* Do you understand?"

"I demand an interview with the prosecutor and a transfer to another cell. If this is not done, I will go on a hunger strike immediately. And I also demand an interview with the commandant."

On the very day of Vojda's arrival in the camp, the commandant had had his trousers stolen from the camp tailor's workshop. It was also a subsidiary duty of the Knight to search for the commandant's trousers. Apart from the fact that the none-too-watchful tailor was now in the next cell, the Knight had no more positive results to show the commandant in the matter of the trousers.

"You have nothing to demand, do you understand? You have nothing to demand . . ." he yelled, and his voice broke.

Vojda waited for a moment, feeling confident and when the color on the Knight's cheeks had receded somewhat, he said: "Excuse me, sir, but those are my rights, guaranteed by the law."

No, the Knight really did not like to hear this kind of talk. Rights. Some rights for these dirty stone-breakers.

"You have no rights, do you understand, *none, none, none!*" He was shrieking hoarsely and jumping about on the spot like a contrary little boy. Only, contrary little boys just want a rocking horse or a clockwork car. The Knight would have liked to kill if he had not been afraid of the responsibility for murder. His morals would have borne it. Anyway, he had never reflected about such concepts as morals. His face was purple again, and his fair hair, eyelashes, and eyebrows contrasted strangely with it. *"I am your right!"*

"I was only sentenced to loss of citizen's rights, sir. I still have my human rights. And my demand is in accordance with the disciplinary regulations. . . ."

The Knight leaped a step forward, seized Vojda by the collar with his left hand and stretched back to hit him with the truncheon in his right hand. Two hundred and fifty pounds of live weight threw itself onto the airman like the torn-off arm of a crane, full of oxlike rage and full of hoarseness: "Rights, I'll give you rights."

Vojda could not withstand this pressure. He did not even have any room to step back. And three or four weeks ago he had weighed

a miserable hundred and fifty pounds. He stretched his hands out
in front of him, his knees crashed against the edge of the bed, and
he began to fall. The Knight's hand flashed into thin air, and, because he was holding onto Vojda's jacket, he followed him down.

Well, this is it, the mess, Vojda thought. He twisted sideways,
felt the brick of the bed under his shoulder blades, seized hold of
the Knight's collar, and then suddenly his feet, in the boots covered
in red slush, came up directly against the lieutenant's face. He saw
the hand with the truncheon tensed for another blow, flinched in-
stinctively, reared up, and kicked out viciously. He felt his heels
strike home, heard the sound of tearing cloth; the collar remained
in his hand. He saw, somehow detached from space, as when loop-
ing the loop, a silhouette with outstretched hands and a truncheon
in one of them falling and flying back into the arms of Coathanger
and the others, who also wavered under the onslaught, with only
the narrowness of the corridor preventing them from falling flat.
Two hundred and fifty pounds are two hundred and fifty pounds.

Vojda became aware of half of the lieutenant's collar and a
piece of sleeve in his clenched fist, and of Hampl standing staring
by the other bed. Of a wire-meshed light somewhere high on the
ceiling. I can still think, he suddenly thought. That's all right. He
was standing up groggily. It's a good thing there's a witness here,
he thought. As long as he doesn't get scared. He's still got a long
time to go. What a man won't do for a year of freedom or a year in
prison! One witness to how a raving prisoner attacked the lieutenant. A trifle.

Someone stepped over the half-lying Knight.

"Comrades," croaked the tattered and mud-covered lieutenant.
Comrades—that was how they used to address one another at the
airfield, and there was said to be freedom and truth in this. Then
he saw Death's-head and Drumstick jumping up onto his bed behind his back. Death's-head held a black baton in his hand, and

more men in uniform with truncheons were crowding in through the door.

He did not try to defend himself. The battle was too unequal. He only wanted to get up and out of the way, but at this moment a truncheon hit him on top of the head. He yelped, threw up his hands as though about to do exercises, but he received another blow on the crown of his head. He turned on one leg and fell to the ground, with his face in the mush in the space between the beds. If he had still been able to think at this moment, it would perhaps have occurred to him that this was really the very end of the matter.

But he knew very little about real things.

He was young. A military pilot educated at military schools. A junior lieutenant.

They stood over him in silence for a moment. Then the two of them fell on Hampl and dragged him off to the next cell with the tailor who had been so careless with the commandant's trousers. No one spoke. No one moved. The two guards came back, lifted Vojda up from the floor, and placed him on the left-hand bed. On his face, the Knight had marks from the heels of the boots together with drops of blood and xylolite mud. He also had a torn collar and only half a sleeve. He walked over to the unconscious Vojda, raised his head, and said:

"Stop pretending! Stop pretending!" He hit him hard on the jaw several times with his fist. "Do you hear! Stop pretending!" He was still breathing heavily. There was also a piece of xylolite stuck on his back. The guards stood around with their truncheons in their hands. In the next cell, Hampl, still wide-eyed with amazement, was beginning to tell the story of the encounter between Vojda and the Knight to the careless tailor and the other occupant of the cell.

"Go for the doctor," said the Knight. They made way for him, and he went out. He was feeling his face with his fingers. He was also rubbing the cut with his index finger. He held the edges of his torn uniform.

Vojda lay limp on his back with his head sideways and his mouth open. One of his hands dangled in the air between the beds.

Coathanger, also still holding his truncheon in his hand, looked at him: "There, you see," he said. "Did you really have to do it?"

Pilot did not hear of all that had happened in the bunker until after parade. Quite a while after parade. They were getting ready for dinner. Today they all had had their leather boots and leggings, but to their surprise the roll call had been completed without a check. It had been a rather makeshift roll call for the Knight.

"Is Havránek here?" asked someone at the door.

"Yes," he replied, and between Pilot and the new arrival a space opened up. It was the medical orderly from sick bay. He had not been in the camp long, and Pilot did not know him. They had never had anything to do with one another.

"That's me," said Pilot.

The medical orderly stopped scanning the faces around him and thrust his way into the space between the bunks.

"Can I sit down?"

"Yes."

"I've got something to tell you." He looked around and lowered his voice. He was obviously afraid. "Vojda sent me. Actually, he hasn't sent me, but they were talking about you over there." He pointed his finger at Havránek's chest.

Pilot examined him suspiciously. Being a medical orderly in sick bay was a soft spot of quite a different kind from his own niche in the mine. People got a soft spot in sick bay by grace of the guards. People who enjoyed their confidence. A spot almost created for fooling, but also for fawning. A medical orderly could change his linen every day, and did not have to appear on parade—he was distributing rations to the people in sick bay. He could bathe himself every day. He really lived comfortably. A medical orderly's spot was above all spots, but there was only one doctor and one medical orderly for the seventeen hundred prisoners in the camp. And the jobs of the medical orderlies were distributed, or rather the job of medical orderly was allocated only to men with good conduct, men who had shown their mettle, usually only to those for whom the mine was no longer safe. A wagon might have crushed them accidentally, or they might have accidentally touched a metal door which was accidentally charged with six hundred volts. This medical orderly had got the job immediately after his arrival in the camp. It was always possible that he had some medical qualification or was in bad health. But a medical orderly could mean an informer. Havránek did not know yet what he was. He could have been.

"What's up?" he asked impatiently.

"Vojda was beaten up in the bunker. He's got a concussion. Death's-head, the Knight, and that other little pisser did it. . . ."

"You mean Coathanger?"

"I think that's what they call him."

"Is Vojda in very bad shape?"

The medical orderly was waiting for Pilot to blurt out and say *what*, or show his astonishment by some gesture. To show his indignation. But nothing of the sort happened. Pilot did, of course, want to say *what*. The sequence of questions that aunts ask little boys on their Sunday visits: What class are you in? Have you always got top marks? Do you do as Mummy tells you? Or, Does Mummy do as you tell her? Or the things you say to girls in a dance hall: Are you from here? I have a feeling we've seen one another somewhere before. You dance so lightly. Is that lady your mother? Are you ever free on Sundays?

The medical orderly did not feel happy about Havránek's mild reaction. As though Pilot were not involved. If he were betrayed, if it came out—with so many people in this dormitory, so many people —that the medical orderly had gone to deliver some messages and pass on some information, it would cost him his soft spot in sick bay. And he had come here for the same reason that had moved Pilot and Vojda. Because of a feeling that something had happened that could not be passed over and wasted. The medical orderly was not a spy, an informer, a *provocateur*. He did not want to earn his parole by doing something dishonorable, and he had not got his job for services rendered or as a gift from the merciful heavens. He had previously worked in a bacteriological laboratory and had slipped out a little quinine for a couple of girls he knew. He had disappointed one of them so much that she had had to confide this fact to the police. But he had also analyzed the blood of some functionary from the Ministry of the Interior when the latter was afraid he had syphilis and did not want to go to his own doctor. And then, when he had the trouble over the quinine, the functionary had at least helped him to get the job as medical orderly.

"He's got a slightly grazed neck, a few bruises, two lumps and a mild concussion. The doctor's with him."

"Our doctor?"

"Ours and the official one. He had him called in."

The prison doctor's decision was also part of the complex element that had moved Pilot, Vojda, the medical orderly, Jarda. . . . The camp doctor was a prisoner like the rest of them, and his number, too, came from the very beginning of the camp.

"What does the doctor say?"

"He hasn't got to the papers yet. You know—you know what I mean, don't you?"

Havránek knew what he meant. He had once been in a similar situation. The medical orderly, too, knew what was involved. The words that a battered man hears when he eventually achieves an official examination: Why are you bothering the doctor when there's nothing wrong with you?

Oh, they knew what he meant.

"Doctor," the man would say and point to the place where he had had a tooth two or three days before.

"I can't see anything" would be the reply from the man with the degree of doctor of universal medicine, a man who had been to university, sworn the academic oath and the doctor's oath to the effect that he would help the suffering. Then he had joined some organization, got a uniform, believed some ideas, anything, and had begun to carry out duties instead of healing and helping. "I can't see anything," he would reply, deliberately overlooking a bruise, a dried-up wound. He would order the escort: "Take him away!"

They knew what he meant.

"Hmm," Pilot murmured. The suspicion was still at work in him, the attempt to be, as far as possible, the sort of person we believe people should be, and at the same time the caution of a man who has experienced how hot bricks can be even when they look perfectly cold. It was not obvious where the catch could be, if there was a catch in it. But he asked: "How was it you came to me particularly?"

"When he was in sick bay, they were drawing up a report on him, a medical one."

Pilot nodded. The medical orderly obviously suffered from epic diffuseness.

"Well, he said the Knight had done it to him because he wanted to be a witness for Tomschin, and he said you were acting as a witness, too. That you came forward together. Anyway, they're talking about it all over the camp."

The medical orderly did not know Pilot. Havránek had never swept the sick bay, and the medical orderly never came to the huts. A disinfection firm from the town used to come and fumigate the insects. *His* suspicion of hot bricks derived precisely from the fact that Pilot had not been put in the bunker, too, even though he had done the same thing as Vojda. He raised his hand and said he saw . . . They were bridging the gulf between them inch by inch, but safely.

"I thought you might be friends. That someone else should know that this had happened in the camp. There was one witness there, someone called Hampl, a juvenile from Kolumbus." Kolumbus was one of the pits that the camp supplied with cheap labor.

"What sort of man is he?"

"He's in for robbery, that's all I know."

"O.K.," said Pilot. "Thanks." He stood up. The medical orderly got up, too. "It was nice of you to come. Thanks. I wouldn't have found out till this evening."

"But how? They're patrolling the bunker."

"Yes," replied Pilot. "Thanks again. Can I do anything for you? Coffee? Tobacco? Food?"

The medical orderly shook his head: "I don't think so."

People usually cannot do too much for one another.

Shortly after, Havránek presented himself at the gate, clean-shaven and spruced up. In his hand, he held his eating dish and a folded towel with his soap, toothbrush, and toothpaste wrapped up in it.

"I'm looking for the shift commander!" he said brusquely to the guard manning the pedal when he stuck his head out of the sliding window of the gatehouse.

"He's in the camp."

Pilot thanked him and turned on his heel, as though he were still wearing the blue battle dress with the Czechoslovakia badge on his sleeve. If the Knight was in the camp, then he could only be in sick bay or in the offices, unless he could be seen, heard, or felt between the huts. He knocked at the door of the first office in the hut behind the gate—the hut that separated the large and small parade grounds. For some unknown reason, it was called number two. The commandant usually allocated the bunkers (only today Dobrovský had got ten days for the parcel of sausage), received requests and complaints (on a fixed day at a fixed time), and again checked the mail the orderly in the office had sorted out for him in advance.

From inside, he heard the Knight shout: "Come in!"

Pilot went in. He came to a halt face to face with the Knight, who was standing up, a junior lieutenant in civilian clothes whose exact function was not known to anyone in the camp, and the commandant. The latter two were sitting at the desk. Pilot and the commandant had known one another for many years. Not only from this camp. Pilot remembered him as quite a young guard, the former tailor just beginning his career years ago in Jáchymov. They both knew what they could expect from one another, and yet they both acted as though they were meeting for the first time, as though they lived and functioned on the pages of a book and their tasks were written and prepared in advance by some third party.

"Very well." The commandant nodded when Pilot had reported. "Well, what do you want, Havránek?"

"Prisoner Vojda was punished by being sent to the bunker, because he saw how the lieutenant here beat prisoner Tomschin." Pilot smiled. "I saw it, too, sir."

They looked at him for a moment. The world was full of traps. The more they saw of it, the less they understood it. Five years ago, and earlier, the commandant would, of course, have shouted out loud and dragged Havránek straight to the bunker and slapped him with his own hands. Only, this was the point—earlier. The commandant had long ago lost his certainty about what the situation would be in a year's time. And being near retirement, he liked to base his life on some pleasant external certainty.

"Just listen to that," hissed the Knight. He leaned his hands on the desk and fixed a piercing gaze on Havránek. If it had not been for the presence of the commandant, he would have exploded long ago.

The commandant looked searchingly at the Knight and Havránek. Inside, he was cursing both of them. He did not wish to be the commandant of a camp that had to be visited by a commission of investigation, and there had been for a long time now no certainty that one of these commissions would not come anyway. And this man Havránek was going home in a few months. God knew how many friends he had. His wife was a singer, and she had not divorced him over all these years. She had a car. God knew all the places he might go to, this man Havránek who had permitted himself to tell the whole parole board to kiss his ass, when the commandant, on direct instructions from above, had proposed him for parole because of good working morale. He put on a tone mildly tinged with melancholy: "Now, look here, Havránek, you already deserve to go to the bunker for the impertinence with which you come here, but—to make things clear to you"—he laughed like a man who is certain of his subject—"Vojda was sent to the bunker for something totally different, you know." He looked happy. "Just so that you know, if you're starting to fight for the rights of the people."

Havránek showed genuine reassurance and reached into his pocket.

"Thank you, sir." He weighed the words carefully, and the eyes of the others hung on his lips. "Then I request you to send this letter through official channels." No one could have said he was smiling. Yet he had on his face something resembling an expression of smiling satisfaction. He put an envelope on the desk in front of the commandant.

The commandant drew the letter toward him across the table and turned it around in his fingers.

"Do you not know that letters are to be handed in open?"

"This one is to a higher institution, sir." On the envelope was the address of the Ministry of the Interior.

The commandant again turned the letter over in his fingers. He looked at it and at Havránek several times.

"It is my duty to convince myself that you are not bothering—this institution—with something I can deal with myself. You understand that, don't you?"

"Not quite clearly, sir."

The commandant stood up and opened the door to the next room.

"Go and wait next door!" he said. He led him through the office, opened the door to another office, let Pilot in, closed the door after him, went back and carefully closed the other door, too. Havránek was left alone. He could not hear a single word of what the three out front were saying to one another. He could only be sure that they were talking about him. And it was not long before the commandant came back. He was alone, and, in his hand, he held the letter. Open.

"You can sit down, Havránek." He motioned him to a chair. "Why did you write this?" He held the letter in front of his face.

Really, why did I write this? I never thought why, Pilot thought. Because of Vojda, whom I don't know? Really. Seriously, sir, you filthy pig—why on earth am I doing it? . . . Then it struck him that it was a pity he could not have been present when the letter was opened and the commandant read it. It must have been most interesting. In the letter, he had mentioned the beating given to Vojda. His man!

He kept quiet.

"After all, this is all lies, Havránek. You're lying like a silly little boy. I've a good mind to punish you. Vojda attacked the lieutenant, do you understand?"

"Yes," nodded Havránek and pursed his lips politely. "You say that, I understand." He knew that all that mattered to the commandant was to appear more sure of himself than he himself did. Since the rehabilitation of traitors and enemies against whom there had been no holds barred, since the time when the most famous and infamous commandants had suddenly themselves ended up behind bars, he had never again felt certain about things. Pilot nodded again. "It happened just as I've written in that letter."

"I beg your pardon, Havránek. I beg your pardon. After all, you know that's not true. Here you are representing Tomschin, and he's given us a statement in which he apologizes to the lieutenant, so that we perhaps won't indict him either and he'll get away with just the bunker. But you state that the lieutenant struck him. Did you see it?"

Yes, Pilot thought to himself. Of course, you won't indict him. None of you will indict him—you're all great humanists. When someone walks into the fence strip and the guard fails to shoot, you punish the guard.

"Yes, I saw it," he said.

"What did you see?" The commandant acted as though he were enjoying it hugely. "What were you able to see?"

"I saw the signs of the blow." That's all you're getting. He would have felt no hatred for the commandant if they had not stood against one another. What he felt for him was not really hatred either. Just a kind of polite rage. The same feeling that had linked him to the crews of the nine German planes he had sent plummeting to the ground or into the sea. He could no longer say how many he had sent to the ground and how many into the sea. But, for a moment, it was the same as it had once been over the Bay of Biscay. He spotted the periscope of a German submarine, a faint white line almost unrecognizable in the waves, which were full of reflected sunlight. Yes, it was a periscope; it was a submarine roughly on the course of the expected convoy, which he was patrolling. He had done nothing but track it and wait for the Liberators to arrive and pour their depth charges onto the spots he had marked with sonar buoys. Mankind is a community of people, and he could do nothing more than drop his sonar buoys with the signalling device in a circle round this presumed, rather than sighted, submarine and wait. Mankind is a community of people, and the men down below in the submarine were people, too, but he knew that their torpedoes were destined for other people, just as the depth charges from the Liberators were destined for other people, and, after all, this war had not been started by Pilot, but by people of the same nation as the crew of the submarine down there, and if there had been no war, he might have been sitting with them somewhere drinking beer, and not dropping buoys around them which would mark them so that death could come more certainly, deliberately and as cheaply as possible.

But now he was not sitting behind the control column of a Typhoon. This time, he had only himself; there had been the woman who wrote him letters, Viceroy and Lucky Strike cigarettes, keepsakes, food in waxed-paper cartons, Praga trucks made under license in England and going well in the Libyan desert. All this he had behind him, even if he was alone. As for the commandant, he had only his tailor's workshop from long ago, his uniform, reminders of using an excessively hot iron, and, most of all, a war swindle and the sewing of braid on Wehrmacht breeches faced with buckskin on the seat. Perhaps this was why he kept silent for so long.

"How do you know about the fight in the bunker?"

If Havránek refused to answer, he would go to the bunker, too. And if he told the truth? It would have been the end of the medical orderly's job. And the end of the medical orderly's trust in Pilot. A bad example for all. If he had to go to the bunker, it had to be for the same thing as Vojda. Only because he had seen the same as Vojda. *I saw the signs of the blow.*

"I heard about it at parade, sir."

"You write about it as a definite fact, and you mention a witness."

Sonar buoys were light tubes less than a pound in weight. Each of them contained a radio probe which gave the position of metal objects in the sea within a certain radius. A submarine is a metal object. The buoys looked like pipes a yard long with an aerial. Underneath was a seal of salt. After a few hours, this dissolved and the buoy became dormant. It must not fall into German hands.

"I do not write about it as a definite fact." Havránek leaned forward and stretched out his hand to the letter. "I've used the expression 'It is said.' "

"Whom did you hear it from? You don't, of course, remember, I suppose?"

"Unfortunately not, sir. I really don't."

The commandant put his index finger on the letter and described a vague ellipse with it on the table: "Listen, Havránek, why are you really doing all this? What are you here for?" He took out a packet of cigarettes and threw them on the table. "Have a smoke."

Havránek smiled. His number was 12. He had been in the camp for many years, and this was not the first time he had spoken to the commandant, even though the commandant had come here only recently and their first encounter had been at Jáchymov, when the commandant had been a mere camp messenger boy, like Bobo or Drumstick or Death's-head were now. Being asked "what for" reminded most people of some unpleasant event, some *faux pas* in life. It shattered their nerves and made them feel uncertain.

"But you know, sir, Operation Stone."

"Ah," the commandant said and made a vague movement with the fingers of both hands, which was supposed to convey that he remembered just a little, though not quite exactly, of course. Operation Stone was a pseudonym, the meaning of which would have been better conveyed by the name: stone cast into water. He scratched his head. "Yes. But really, Havránek, why are you doing this? Do you think I'll get into trouble?" He flicked the torn envelope. It flew across the desk and stopped against the inkwell.

Why I am doing it is hard to explain to you, you jerk, if you don't know for yourself. *Getting into trouble,* you representative of the new and juster world. You sewing-machine revolutionary in a uniform with the ten years' service ribbon on the chest, you revolutionary on the verge of retirement with your bonuses for every ton of coal the prisoners dig out. I don't give a damn for your *getting into trouble,* though I would welcome it. Pilot smiled and remained silent. Then he cleared his throat and said: "You know, sir, I've been re-educated here, and I read somewhere that under socialism people are not beaten up. That it's a progressive doctrine and a just social order. . . ."

The commandant shook his head in despair. Then he stood up and walked around the desk. He stopped in front of Havránek. "Do you insist that I send it?" He looked at Pilot over an index finger raised in warning. "Think about it!"

Yes, *yes,* this was the routine: think about it! Vacillate. It raised a smile. At that time, *at that time*—Operation Stone. They had been specialists. During his stopover at Zurich, two gentlemen had devoted themselves to him. They spoke quite correct English. Then they decided that they might just as well speak Czech, and swapped stories about home. There was a lot of it, and these *provocateurs* had later given evidence about it against him, but none of this could be supported by any firm proof. Not that the court really needed firm proof, this gloomy bench of men carrying out tasks in the sector of justice. Anyway, he no longer remembered it either—the bottle of imported Martell cognac as a means of espionage. Pilot had stopped caring for his own personal justice the moment he understood that these two men and many others did their jobs only in order to prove how necessary they were. They were paid to give protection against enemies, and Pilot's conviction was not the activity in which they would have imagined themselves. If there had been no enemies, then they would have had to fabricate some. Pilot had had enough of the one war he had fought, while people like this commandant had been profiteering with cloth in exchange for dripping. He had twice jumped into the sea from a burning aircraft and had been lucky to be found relatively soon by the seaplane from Air Sea Rescue. No, that war had been no fun, nor had he fought for the fun of it, but because there was nothing else he could do. If a man could fly, England gave him a plane. That was all there was to it. He had not learned to smoke a pipe there, and he continued to eat his main meal at midday. *Think about it.* If he wanted to think about it, he did not have to do so in the commandant's office. Just whom did they think they were testing, whom did he think he was testing? . . . this commandant with his cheap trick of the proffered cigarette?

Pilot took out his tobacco tin and slowly and carefully rolled himself a cigarette.

"Smoke, there are cigarettes here."

He shook his head without a word and licked the cigarette paper with his tongue.

"I would like it to be sent off, sir."

The commandant nodded.

"All right. I'll send it." He knew he would not.

Pilot stood up. He knew that the audience was over. He, too, knew that the commandant would not send it. The letter would never leave the camp. Or even the commandant's office.

"Look here, aren't you sorry . . ." The ruler of the camp again walked around the desk, this time to the other side, opened the drawer and dropped the paper in. "After all, you could have been home by now. You're working against yourself." He closed the drawer with his knee and looked Pilot in the eye: "I'll admit it to you, if you want." He smiled and nodded his head over his shoulder in the direction of the door of the outer office. "The lieutenant, O.K., I'll admit to you that perhaps all that you think of him . . . but you are still working against yourself. You won't break the wall with your head. After all, you could have been home long ago!"

Against himself. Home. Freedom, women, love-making. And: Let the young lady plug her ears, and you gentlemen can kiss my ass (one, two, and three). The commandant remembered that business only too well.

"Against yourself, Havránek. Do you understand me?"

"Yes, sir, certainly, I understand." Against himself. A man had to work against himself to some extent if he wanted people to be for him. Against himself. Many people had died in order to be such. Better people than you are, commandant. Against himself? No. Just that he was not a wily one who kept to the wall and did deals with dripping while better men fought. But was it worth talking about this *now, here?*

"Perhaps you wouldn't understand, sir," he said. That a man must long for a life without walls to be breached. Walls like a bald fat man dressed in creased trousers, with his pockets neatly ironed. Or that he could not leave Vojda where he was, because of a whole complex of unwritten, incomprehensible, and unnamed principles of decency. The commandant was on a different wave length, on a different track. Perhaps he, too, would have been decent if there had been an order telling him to be. If he had not been bitterly aware of this smallness. But even in all this, he would have contrived to remain a cheap trickster.

They looked at one another.

"You're not a Communist, are you, Havránek? You don't think —" he cleared his throat and assumed an ironical tone—"you don't think that you are passing some judgment on yourself when you address yourself to a place where there are Communists? Communists like me . . ."

A Communist. You went into the Party because it was the thing to do after the war—it promised a career and meant risking nothing, my lad.

"I am a citizen of this country, sir—and Vojda, too, is a Communist, just like you, but that did not seem to matter to the lieutenant."

"It's difficult to talk to you, Havránek. I tell you nothing happened in the bunker."

"I think you are badly informed, sir." Now Pilot was smiling just as he had the day before, when he came forward to the Knight as a witness. "I request you to arrange an interview with the prosecutor."

There were Communists at the Ministry, the commandant was a Communist, the prosecutor was a Communist, Vojda was a Communist. Only those at the top answered for their power. They answered for the laws that they themselves drafted. All the rest was double talk and fooling. Tomschin had been in the right, Vojda had been in the right, despite the fact that Tomschin had tried to cross the frontier illegally and Vojda had run a man down with alcohol in his blood. He, too, Havránek, was in the right with his letter, in the right as far as the regulations stated in black and white in all the corridors of all the huts in the camp. There were a hundred and one other rights and truths, but none of them so clear. They could drop it, but then they would have to admit—not only the commandant, but all the others, too—today and every day that they were liars, that they did not recognize their own laws that they had given for themselves as Communists and which as Communists they had given to this country that they ruled. They would have to admit this to him, Havránek.

The commandant said:

"Wait a moment!" He sat down behind the desk and rested his elbows on it.

Yes, Pilot thought to himself. I'm going for you now. I'm doing
all this partly in order to get you. If you had the power and courage at this moment, you would kill me. But I'm fed-up to the teeth
with you. Right up to the teeth. With the way you and all like you
have made shit of every truth and every ideal. All those like you
who recognize only what they do as right, and then force everyone
else to recognize it as well. But you probably have no thoughts
about that. You just drink vodka and brandy and do everything in
such a way that they can carry on undisturbed, and you haven't
even the courage to stand behind your own watchdogs. He realized
it was just as well he had only made a fleeting reference to Hampl.
They would work him over with all their might, of course. They
would have done so anyway, but now they would be less patient
and perhaps ruin it and overdo it.

"Permission to go, sir?"

"Wait," repeated the commandant. It was his battle, too.
"You've been here so long, Havránek. You'll be out in four or five
months, won't you?"

"Yes."

"Well, you see, do you think all this is going to do you any
good?" He hit the desk with the back of his hand. "Do you think I
don't know how you've been thinking all these years of turning the
tables and getting your revenge on *us*? But you see, *we* are still
here, and you are leaving your life here. You could go home within
two weeks, Havránek. Home. You know it only too well." The
commandant wanted to be right. To be right in his own way. The
card on which he had staked his money when he left tailoring and
took up this jail trade had been a good one, after all. It was a
trump, it had been a trump for more than fourteen years now.
Perhaps this man, who had spent so much time in this place, did
not understand this. In this place, where he was underground so
much of the time.

Pilot remained silent.

"Havránek, I offer to cancel all these things and withdraw the indictments against Vojda and Tomschin. I can do that, you know, don't you? But tell me why. Why are you doing all this? Prison comradeship? What does that matter to you? Don't you realize you've lost? And then that business with your parole . . . You've lost everything, do you understand? Just see that!"

Pilot shrugged his shoulders lightly.

"I think I'm right, sir. And being right is quite a good thing, even here."

"You think you're right? You? But you're not."

"I think I am."

They fell silent for a moment again. It seemed unending, though it did not last more than a minute or two. The commandant sat behind the desk, leaning slightly forward and resting his elbows on the flat surface. His hands lay straight beside one another.

Havránek stood, cap in hand, in front of the chair he had been sitting on a moment before.

It seemed that the commandant was thinking of something else. But then he simply raised his hand and turned slightly toward the window, so that he presented an almost pure profile to Pilot. He looked outside, at the corner guard tower with its large windows and the two shooting holes along it at floor level. For prisoners, the greatest bait was the thought of going home. Someone, somewhere, for reasons that were unknown to the commandant and that disturbed him, had once come up with the bright idea of settling the Havránek case quietly by releasing him on parole. The commandant had agreed, but it had all gone wrong. The bait obviously had no effect on Pilot. The commandant was not ready to suffer another blot on his record. He turned his head to the prisoner.

"Well, off you go," he said.

Havránek went.

"Prisoner Havránek dismissing, sir!"

Soon after, all the guards, including the one who was now on constant watch at the bunker, were distracted by Daniel. He came to report, to inform, that there was a fight in hut six. The guards, full of their sense of duty, and also welcoming this distraction from a duty that was extremely boring, went into the hut and the dormitory indicated and began to investigate eagerly. In vain, as almost always, so that it did not surprise them at all, and they believed all the more that there really had been a fight. Fights were part of the normal camp life.

This time, too, no one knew anything about any fight, everyone had a perfect alibi, no one remembered anything, and, in the end, they began to beg quite ridiculously for coal, which had not been issued for more than a week now. There was something like good humor in the atmosphere. Extremely good humor, an atmosphere in which they all enjoyed themselves. It affected the guards, too. Even Death's-head. They stood in the middle of the room like a troupe of cabaret comedians.

"I'll give you coal! Don't place your orders here! Now, how was it with that fight?" These prisoners, these prisoners here were as cunning as foxes, and you had to be on your guard against them all the time so they didn't make a fool of you. So you didn't look a fool. "We'll find out anyway, as quick as you like. Own up. If you confess, you get less punishment!" Death's-head slapped his open hand with his folded gloves, wearing the smiling expression of a man who never admits defeat. He even seemed to feel like laughing.

By this time, Jarda had opened the door of the first cell in the bunker by means of a broomstick. It seemed impossible, but it worked. The cell was not empty. The enraged Knight had spent the whole afternoon coming across other prisoners who grinned, and all the cells were full. Crammed full. Overfilled. Only Vojda was alone, in number nine. At the grille, Pilot was speaking to Günther: "Everything all right?"

"Yes."

"The commandant told me you tried to apologize to the Knight."

Günther spat into the corridor. He was a simple Sudeten German soul: "He's bluffing. He told me that if I apologized to the lieutenant, they'd forget about it all."

"Did he ask you?"

"No."

There was a crowd of people around, handing bread, cigarettes, pieces of blanket on belts, shirts, to their friends inside. A man needs ridiculously little in order to live and to feel a certain contentment. Bread, cigarettes, an extra shirt, a piece of blanket wrapped around his body under his jacket. A feeling that, even amid the greatest persecution, he would still manage to find a moment for himself.

Vojda pushed his way up to the grille. He shook hands with Pilot. For the first time since they had known one another. Vojda was moved.

"Is it true?" asked Pilot.

Vojda nodded and smiled without saying a word. He had been laughing since the moment he had heard the voices and noise behind the doors. It was like the anxiety of a young man before his first night with a woman. *Is she real?* He seized the bars and Havránek's hands with his own hands. He had been through a beating, he had grown up a bit. He had now become a man with something to remember. It was like a decoration. He was assimilated to the world in which he had to live. He had a place in it. Not some vague fiction from a Party meeting. Not the black-and-white conception of a keen television viewer. They had taken him to and from sick bay on a string like a circus animal, and all the time he had sensed danger circling round him. No, that just is not done, he kept repeat-

ing in his mind every minute. His faith in Pilot was the heaviest
weapon in his arsenal. He was glad it had been rewarded. It had
become the bridge to a world that had seemed completely lost when
he was lying half-frozen and curled up on the bed in number nine.
The moment when a plane detaches itself from the ground, the
dizzying feeling of climbing into the sun, the calm and brightness
over the cloud front, the warrant officers from air-traffic control
who had liked his hair. Love affairs that had dragged on from nothing to nothing to the sounds of Satchmo's trumpet and hoarse voice.

Somewhere in some unknown office, an indifferent typewriter
was perhaps right now tapping out the catalogue of his crimes.
Somewhere in the prosecutor's office, a phone was perhaps ringing.

"What will they do?" he asked.

"They'll put in an indictment against you, saying you attacked
him. That's the way they always do it."

Indictment and sentence. An official voice pronouncing the
number of unending days with parades in leggings and leather
boots. Wages in worn camp money, lumps of oatmeal dropping to
the bottom of the dish. Hardening fat on badly cooked peas full of
stones.

"Keep calm! It has to work this time!" Pilot squeezed Vojda's
hand. He did not completely believe all he was saying. But he was
willing to do anything. There was not very much left that he could
do. Lies indeed have short legs, but they sometimes have danger-
ously long hands and are indifferent to their legs.

"I am calm," said Vojda. "Completely calm!" The doctor had
diagnosed a slight concussion and nervous shock. His hands were
shaking. The shaking had come over him while he was unconscious,
aided, too, by the icy cold in the bunker that he had tried to over-
come without success.

"Keep calm. Don't let yourself be bluffed and stand your
ground," Pilot repeated. He spoke in the knowledge of letters which
were already written and which, inside his leggings, were waiting to

be handed over to a civilian miner somewhere in the darkness of
the pit. Jarda had copies of them. But he still needed the certainty
of someone to inquire about their fate from the outside. "Have you
got anyone outside who could put in a complaint in your name?
Parents, fiancée, friend? Someone you trust completely?"

Vojda shook his head slowly. He was a little ashamed. He had
no one. Going to bed together over a Satchmo record—that was not
trust and love, just some happy game that everyone played, and no
one thought the worse of them for it. Comrades at the airfield.
Meetings in the Party organization. They resolved that they would
put in one thousand hours of work on the construction of a children's playground, that they would do this and that. What were
they supposed to resolve this time? He did not know what to ask
them. The name of the senior lieutenant with whom he shared his
room in the airfield quarters for unmarried officers came into his
head. They had each vacated it for the night whenever one of them
needed it for himself. He had lent him his Satchmo record, for
those occasions when music was needed.

"I have got a friend at the airfield. . . ." The friend of a man
who had been locked away. It threw a bad light on him. It had
been with him that Vojda had had that drink before the crash that
had cost a human life. Vojda was not certain that he himself would
have done it if the situations had been reversed. That is, whether he
would have done it without knowing about the Knight, the beating,
the machine-gun towers, and cell number nine. It was much simpler
not to complicate your life, to have money, and to go out occasionally after duty to the air-traffic control with a bar of candy in your
pocket. Their duty was to fly, and not to take upon themselves the
cares and worries of other people. What would he have done if the
situations had been reversed? What?

"Do you think he'll do something for you?" asked Pilot.

Vojda again realized that he was not convinced of it. To act, to extinguish something that was not burning him personally, to burn his fingers. To engage in a lone battle. How? With what? For what? And against whom? "I don't know," he said. "I can't think of anyone else." He threw up his sticky hands. "It's the only chance."

Pilot knew of no other either. The woman who sang in a night-club and wrote him letters that he destroyed could do nothing about it. Nothing at all officially—human relationships without personal contact are not recognized by the law. And unofficially? Only very little, even if Pilot, of course, asked her to try.

"O.K." He shook his head. "Write the address down for me!" He pushed a pencil and a piece of paper through the bars. "On here." It was the only chance. For himself, Pilot thought there was nothing he had forgotten and nothing else he could have done. Of course. Nothing was over. The sonar buoys were dropped, and you only had to sit back and keep the memory alive. There was chance, fate, happiness. He knew enough about them already, and he believed that they mostly worked against man. Especially when they are not accompanied by any knowledge of love. The woman who wrote him letters was perhaps at this very moment singing in the red glare of the footlights. Somewhere a car had crashed. From the love of people just at this moment, a child would grow who would commit manslaughter in twenty years. The man at the airfield . . .

"Ludvík, this man," he pointed to the paper, "is he a Communist?"

"Yes."

"Can he write a complaint as a Communist?"

"I don't know."

"Will he do it?"

"Is it the only chance?"

"That's just what I was thinking a moment ago."

Vojda thought for a moment. Political training, obligations for brigade hours. The mess. The other bed vacated. That was one side of the coin. And the other?

"I think he'll do it."

Havránek nodded: "Good. I'll go now. Keep your chin up!" Then he turned to the throng around him: "Scram, boys, before someone comes!" He watched them disappearing gradually into the yard and the huts. Someone else ran across the corridor with a piece of substitute salami from the camp canteen and pushed it through to the hooligans in number one, who were closing up the cells: "Give this to Doubek in number four!"

An angular cherub with a tattooed arm opened number four again and disappeared inside. Doubek put his head out and said thank you.

"That's all now, come on," said Pilot a little impatiently. The action had mushroomed, and everyone with a friend in the bunker had wanted to take advantage of it. But the investigation of the fight in hut six could not go on forever.

The donor of the salami stood beside Pilot, breathing heavily: "I thought I'd never make it." He pointed to the corridor. "Hope he'll be all right. He's my *friend*."

Pilot nodded at him. The cherub again checked the bolts on all the cells, made a face at them, and banged the door of number one behind him.

Havránek took the broomstick with the wire loop at the end into his hand, caught the handle of the bolt and pulled it.

Jarda came up: "All right?"

"Yes, it was easy."

It was not only a question of justice. Of some confrontation. What was at stake was a feeling of life that still had some chance left beyond the frame it had been forced into. For a world that should still have some chance left and as few frames as possible.

The camp loud-speakers spluttered and hissed a dozen names. Including Dobrovský's. A new consignment for the bunker.

I hope they put them in together, Pilot thought to himself. He felt very tired. He longed for a roll and a piece of Danish cheese. He might, of course, just as well have longed for Sophia Loren. Both existed. And there were men who proclaimed they would give three years of their lives for one night with Lollobrigida.

"How about getting some sleep?" he said to Jarda. They left the grille by the bunker and, carrying the broomstick, dragged themselves wearily to the hut. In the entrance, they met the guards who had been summoned to the fight. Their mission had ended, and they were leaving after an unsuccessful search.

In the turn of the corridor stood Daniel, uninvolved and charming as Mephistopheles. Their eyes met, and Pilot and Jarda took off their caps, as the regulations said, and stood still until the uniformed group with truncheons in their hands had passed them.

"Good night, sir," said Jarda softly, and Drumstick, who heard him and assumed the greeting to be addressed to him, replied casually: "Good night."

Jarda had at last handed in the completed slogan that afternoon.

INCREASE YOUR WORK EFFORT! YOU WILL SHOW BY YOUR WORK THAT YOU ARE WORTHY OF BECOMING A FULLY FLEDGED MEMBER OF HUMAN SOCIETY!

The lettering was bright red and light blue, on a yellow, slightly cadmium-colored background. It did strike Drumstick that the slogan could in fact have been expanded to read FULLY FLEDGED AND VALID. That sounded better and more elaborate to him. In the final analysis, he was responsible for educational work among the prisoners. But he needed the poster to hang up by the next day—he had promised the commandant at some meeting about education. It was to be put up on the small parade ground, right behind the gate, so that the prisoners would have it in view every day as they left for work and returned from work. The joiners in the camp workshop had already made a frame for the poster and a wooden top for

protection against the rain. All of them, of course, like Jarda, had
done this voluntarily. In the interests of their re-education.

Yes.

Work is the mother of progress.

SIX

final reckoning

Nunc dimittis servum tuum   *—A classic*

. . . and behind the door which was still swinging stood a man in a sweat-stained buckskin shirt. Silence fell, broken only by the squeak of the door hinges. Then they, too, were quiet. It was one of Shilby's men whom they had been pursuing two days before through Fork Canyon. Now he had a Colt in his hand, and they were powerless against him.

But he spun it on its trigger guard and handed it to Gatsby butt first:

"I respect the law, sheriff," he said.

Some time after this, the Knight sat in the inn that stood opposite the mine. The pit was a hundred and fifty years old, but the inn had stood there even before that. It was said that the shaft had been sunk here because of the inn, so that the miners would not have far to go for their beer.

It was a midsummer noon. The morning shifts had not knocked off yet—only a few firemen and gangs who worked in hot parts of the coal face and thus had a shortened shift. The inn was almost empty. People did not go for a beer before the afternoon shift. Nor before the morning one. Going for a beer before work was the privilege of the night shift.

On a long bench by the wall sat several pensioners who had grown accustomed to coming here just as they had once clocked in at the mine. When you had no more work to fill your life, the inn was a pretty good place.

The Knight was in civilian clothes. He was not waiting for a shift to start. He had nothing at all to say to any of the escorts or prisoners. He was waiting for the afternoon bus. He was leaving. He had got another transfer.

The cage came up. They saw the spinning spokes of the huge wheels over the shaft slow down and then stop. At the back, by the extraction shaft, the sorting gear whirred. The escort guards sat in the sun outside the clocking-in shed, sunbathing, with their machine pistols between their knees.

One of them went off to the cage and returned a moment later with three men in khaki with blue bands. The two outer men were supporting the middle one, who had an injured head that had been bandaged somewhere down below with an emergency dressing. They walked away slowly, with the escort guard behind them, in the direction of sick bay. The escort saw the Knight, and the Knight saw the escort, but they did not exchange so much as a nod.

"Got it on the head. Not too bad if he's still walking!" The pensioner beside the Knight waved his hand and drew on his pipe. They were all typical old miners, worn out, marked by the mine, by many, many years in the mine. Crisscrossed with wrinkles, indifferent to the dangers of the depths. Used to chewing tobacco and accustomed to man's insignificance in the face of the hundred and one dangers that may be lurking below ground. Yet perhaps not a single one of them would have chosen any other job, if he had been able to be twenty or thirty years younger and make the decision again.

The Knight agreed. It did not look like a serious injury. A piece of coal. Perhaps a rock that had slipped from the raised conveyer belt. A careless wave of someone's pick.

"You used to be here in the camp, weren't you?" a voice asked him.

The Knight looked at the speaker. It was a little old man, completely wrinkled and with a swollen gland on his neck. A million wrinkles with ingrained dirt on his cheeks. Dull-white blocked pores with a red spot in the middle of his nose.

"Yes," he said.

"And you're giving up the work now, are you?"

The Knight drank his beer.

"Yes," he replied hoarsely. It was not true. He was only leaving for another camp. "I helped a couple of people," he said pensively and released the handle of his glass. He let his hand fall onto the table in a gesture of powerlessness. He knew what was good for little old men, and, for a moment, he saw himself just as he wished to see himself and as he wished to be seen. Great, powerful, just, humiliated, but unscathed. "Then someone threw the book at me." He repeated the vain gesture against the wickedness of the world with his hand and drank again. He also knew that nothing was good for these little old men. For some reason, they were always closer to the prisoners than to the guards. As though they were linked by some connecting path. And all those other phrases taken from the May 1st editorials of the papers! These men had worked all their lives and had always been closer to those who worked than to those who merely guarded them.

The old man nodded his head. The gland on his neck swelled and receded. Everyone around was listening to them, and he was conscious of the seriousness of the moment.

"What people do today," he said. He would quite certainly have gone on to tell them about the difficulties he had in his retirement, but just at this moment the siren on the tower began to hoot, announcing the end of the shift. The steam vanished in the sunlight above the hoots, an evaporating cloud. The siren drowned their voices and attracted their attention completely. The Knight's bus came in, too.

The lieutenant drank again and went to pay at the bar, where the surly barman was doing a crossword puzzle. The Knight was in civilian clothes and almost like a normal man.

At about the same time, Havránek and Vojda were sitting on the low wall that bounded the steps to the cookhouse. Their shift was on nights this week, but the sun had drawn them out of bed. You could not waste such weather in sleeping, it would have been a sin, even if it were possible to get to sleep at all in the heat of the huts with the sun beating down on them. They also had too much to say to one another or to be silent about together to be able to afford the time wasted sleeping.

Of course, all the credit belonged to the weather. Even the guards respected it, although prisoners sitting around in the yard usually obstructed them in something and they always drove them back into the huts or to do some job or other. This time, they left them in peace.

The door to the workshops of the camp management was open. Outside a door, a tapping shoemaker sat at his bench, which had been carried out into the open, and through a door farther down, the tailor, in a white civilian coat, was seen moving about in the gloom of the room. He was new and very eager. The old tailor had not been allowed to return after the incident of the commandant's trousers and had ended up as a breaker in the pit. The trousers had never been found. The commandant's trousers.

"Tomorrow, then!" said Vojda. A little unnecessarily. He knew he was saying it a little unnecessarily. Everyone knew it was tomorrow. This *tomorrow* belonged to Pilot. He was leaving the camp.

"That's right," he agreed. The days of every one of us are numbered in one way or another. The creatures in the camp, the hut people, counted the days like the time elapsed since Thermidor. So and so many days behind them, and so and so many days ahead. The world of Year One. In 37, but also perhaps in 4,522. Pilot could now say in 1!

"I'll be going home just a year after you." They had also said this to one another many times before.

"A year." Pilot looked at the dust at his feet and then at the blue sky. "A year isn't a long time. One more winter, one Christmas, one spring—and you'll be sitting like I am today. It's only many years . . ." It was like the proverb "Many dogs are a hare's death." His seven and a half years here appeared like a cemetery wall. Seven and a half years. Was it at all possible? It robbed him of speech and thought. He, too, had behind him the time when he had thought it possible to swap the remaining years of his life for one night with Lollobrigida. They all had it behind them. The phonies and the honest men. The charlatans and the heroes.

"What will you do?"

Pilot shrugged his shoulders. He knew why Vojda was asking him the same things so many times over. In a year, he would be thinking about these things himself, and he was probably thinking about them even today, and in a year—just as now—he would still find no satisfactory answer. But perhaps things with a perfectly satisfactory answer do not exist. "Something—somewhere," he said softly. "Or somewhere something. First of all, whatever comes my way, and then whatever I feel like."

"Is it all over with the flying?"

Havránek laughed.

Of course, it was all over with the flying. To hell, he was still asking questions as stupidly as an old lady about the mysteries of the telephone. Over and over, several times over. Everything uprooted. First, because of all that seven and a half years meant for an employee and representative living from the evaluation of people as they paraded for work. Secondly, because of all that seven and a half years meant for an airman and all he needed to know in order to be able to fly—it had already gone from Pilot's memory. Thirdly, because of the years that had added themselves to his age. The fourth, fifth, sixth, seventh and a whole pile of other reasons in a long line, so that they could be stacked behind one another if the need arose.

"You're speaking like a boy," he said. Ludvík, of course, would never go back to his unit and he knew it, but Pilot was not so cruel as to remind him that he, too, was one of those infected with the plague, not so much because he had caused a crash in which a man had died, as because he was *here,* and being here meant something like being infected with the plague, for this society in which they

lived, for this land which they loved in spite of everything. He
knew of the things he should be thinking about, but to his surprise
he did not think about them. One more night. Two more roll calls.
Sunset and sunrise on the gray horizon of the camp. Then the
woman from the nightclub sitting behind the wheel of her car,
which would be waiting outside the gate from early morning. Exhibited and exhibiting herself, as always on any of those rare visits.
I am only for the man I'm waiting for. Only for him, you others,
only for you, darling. What would she say? Tell me?—or, You
don't need to say anything! And she would put her hand over his
mouth. What was her complexion like now? Seven years of singing
under the grease paint in the red spotlights—that left its mark.

He rolled himself a cigarette slowly and attentively, as always,
and then passed the tobacco tin and papers to Vojda. In fact, it
wasn't even his any more. He had promised it to Ludvík. He had
promised and in some cases already handed over all of his private
possessions in the camp. Tomorrow, he would go into the civilian
clothing store in his hessian outfit, which he had to hand in, and put
on his old but still good suit, which the woman had sent him
two weeks ago. How often he had changed clothes into another
life, another reality. Into a Polish uniform in September 1939. Into
a French one two months later. Into an English one a year after
that. Into a Czechoslovak one in 1945. Into the colors of the airline. And then into this hessian suit of prison gray.

"Would you like to go abroad? To England?"

A piece of his life had remained in England, and it had been a
good life. He did not think, nor could he think, anything bad about
it. But if you could endeavor to achieve something at home and live
at home, then it was better to do it here. It was possible, even in
this camp and from this camp. He would never have engaged in the
duel with the Knight and everything the Knight represented unless
he had believed in this possibility.

"No," he said and shook his head, even though he believed that no question in the world could be answered unambiguously. No question had an exhaustive answer. Explain how you like me. How much? Show me?

The commission of investigation had arrived. Vojda's friend had not thrown Pilot's letter away, but had handed it on to the Party organization of his, and Vojda's former, unit, and the organization had sent out photocopies of the complaint in all directions. It was also the only letter that achieved what they wanted, although Pilot had sent out several via the civilian miner. To ministries, offices, and commissions attached to offices. But the Party organization of an elite military unit had to be given a straight answer. And so a commission of investigation had arrived, and things had got moving, even though the first question Pilot was asked had been: How did you send this letter off?

"I don't know," he had said. "I had no stamps, and I left it lying on the table when I went to work, intending to mail it the next day, but it got lost."

They did not believe him, of course, but he had long ago ceased to bank on belief and disbelief. To rely on them as a yardstick of purity and rightness. Belief, to rely on the brain that invented it and which I acknowledge as better than my own? Belief was not important. Hampl was important—he had not traded in his sense of jail honor as a thief and robber for the phantom of early parole (on the recommendation of the camp commandant—Discipline, Work, Conduct), a phantom that the commandant really was in a position to conjure up. And there was a damned lot of difference between living in the camp for three more years like an unloved child who has caused trouble by his testimony, a man whom we remember and whom they remember, and spending six months of relative peace and quiet here, waiting to go before the board and then going there with the feeling that the same day you would be outside the wire.

Also important was the broomstick with the wire loop at the

end, with which Jarda had managed to open the door of the first cell in the bunker. So was that friend of Vojda's from the airfield, whose address Pilot had got from Vojda at the cell and who felt as they did, although he had a quiet life, money, and a secure position, although he did not need to risk anything, although he had within him no knowledge of the camp as a concept that accompanied him everywhere he went. This one letter out of all those Pilot had sent off had set the wheels of the machine in motion, so that in the end the Knight was at least transferred and got another line or cross in his cadre record. Laws are intended to be valid, and all else was only a game, the outcome of which he knew very well once they had started to play it according to the rules. Almost according to the rules. The secret lay in forcing the regulations to assume validity, and in forcing the others to begin to play. Otherwise, of course, nothing had changed. They continued to live in the camp. The turnstile at the gate went on counting the prisoners in and out, on the strength or off the strength. Bobo went on longing for the unfulfilled dream of his destiny as a military messenger, which had been denied him. No one had proved that the commandant had suppressed Pilot's letter to the Ministry. They never saw Tomschin again. He had escaped from the camp by night, straight from the bunker to freedom, and he had only been able to send them a message via the miners about his drinking bout in the nearest inn.

Some of the guards had dropped their progressive progressivity. The Knight had been transferred. First, he had stopped serving as shift commander and appeared only on watch in the towers, and then he disappeared altogether. It was said that, for some time, he would have a certain percentage deducted from his pay. Rumors put out by the camp accounts office. No one ever communicated anything more precise to Havránek, Vojda, or Tomschin, or even to Vojda's—now former—unit's Party organization about this.

But Vojda's triumvirate of Discipline-Work-Conduct was

ruined, and he would now have to serve the full eighteen months. In their entirety.

Pilot struck a match and held it to his cigarette and to Vojda's. Vojda had very quickly learned to smoke here, just as people quickly learn all pleasant vices. The match burned with a scarcely visible white flame in the sunlight even when he threw it down, and it curled up into a black cinder on the sand under their feet.

"Would you have run away if you'd known they were going to lock you up?"

"Out of the country, you mean?"

"Yes, perhaps to England. You have friends there, people you know."

"Run away? Perhaps I would have. Yes, I think so." If he had known that seven and a half years awaited him. There is always some "if" that we do not know about in advance. And there were other things here, too. The woman, his firm base, had waited all through the war for him, and this time there was no hope that she could go on waiting for anything so exact as the end of a war. He would have run away. He would probably have been flying for some airline company now. There were also his nine planes shot down and a number of decorations. Perhaps he would have been flying and not sitting here today with Ludvík Vojda. He stretched out his foot and crushed the black matchstick into the dust with his heel. There was also a thing called patriotism.

"I had no reason for running away."

Between them was the gulf of two lives spanned by a single bridge. Joint possession of things and joint possession of this country which they also knew so deep down inside, wherever the mine passages reached. The fact that, jointly, they did not want anything except what really belonged to them. Being honest is a terrible thing. Like being just. Most people, though they want to be both honest and just, also want something out of it—despite the fact that these two things together give the feeling of an unreconciled soul.

The world had a face of its own. Havránek was calm, and Vojda was also calm. Perhaps it would not have needed much for them to have been looking at one another on the screens of radar scanners. It was a strange accident. They had to meet the Knight, to descend eight hundred yards below ground, to feed on boiled beans, and waste their lives, the only lives they had, but nonetheless it seemed that God was man's comrade. They had made friends and were now sitting together, though they would never go fishing together or to an inn with a familiar bartender, and it was probable that they would never see one another again. Nonetheless, they would live in the knowledge of one another, somewhere on this earth, the knowledge of a man we know is *our* man. Where there is more courage, more sense of responsibility, there is always more truth. Solidarity, laws, justice—all sorts of tricks can be played with all this. Words from the encyclopedia. Words whose true worth we do not know.

"Are you looking forward to it?" Vojda should, of course, have said, "to getting home," but Pilot knew what he meant.

"What sort of question is that?"

"It's a stupid question."

"That's what I thought, too."

They laughed.

Bobo stopped beside them. They stood up to show him the prescribed respect, but he motioned them down again with his hand: "Sit down, sit down." And then he said: "Nice today, isn't it? It's cleared up."

Havránek nodded assent. "It's cleared up, sir."

"It's your turn in a few days, isn't it?"

"In one day. Tomorrow."

"Well, so it's all over. Hope you enjoy yourself."

"Thanks."

"You'll be at the swimming pool by this time tomorrow, will you?"

"Perhaps, if I haven't forgotten how to swim."

Bobo sighed. "Originally, I wanted to be on the road, with the motorcycle men, you know. . . ."

It was the old, oft-heard story of the mistake in life of a romantic youth who had made a bad bet and had a bad tip.

"That will all sort itself out, you'll see, sir."

Bobo cheered up. "Do you think so?"

"Definitely!"

"They told me I had to serve two years here first, and then they'd give me a transfer."

"Well, there you are."

"But I've been here three years now."

"Maybe it's got held up somewhere along the line."

Bobo, too, lit a cigarette and took off his cap.

They smoked without movement, without thought. They half closed their eyes against the sun. Calm, weak, sleepy, quite uncertain. The hot air wavered over the asphalt roofs of the huts.

"At least one has some hope," said Bobo. "If I thought I'd be rotting away here forever, I'd probably go mad."

ABOUT THE AUTHOR

Jan Beneš was born in Czechoslovakia on March 26, 1936. He began his career as an artist and sculptor and in 1958 won a gold medal for toy design at Expo 58 in Brussels. He worked as a miner, a taxi driver and a theater technician until 1962 when he had his first story published in Prague. His stories have since appeared in England, France, Germany, and Italy.

Known as one of the most active champions of literary freedom in the Czechoslovak Writers' Union, he earned the displeasure of the authorities in 1965 when, on being refused a passport without explanation, he filed a law suit against the Minister of the Interior for infringing his constitutional rights. In 1966, he collected more than 300 signatures from fellow writers for a protest petition against the imprisonment of the Soviet writers Andrei Sinyavski and Yuli Daniel. Soon afterwards he was arrested and spent 11 months in custody while the Czech secret police pieced together "evidence." After a 1,200 page indictment was compiled, the police invented additional charges of a common criminal nature to enable the prosecutor to present the case in court. He was sentenced to five years in prison in 1967 and was pardoned in 1968 by President Novotny—Novotny's last official act before being succeeded by Dubçek.

This book was set on the linotype in Old Style No. 7
Composition, printing, and binding by
H. Wolff Book Mfg. Co., New York, New York.
Designed by Jacqueline Schuman